Out of Office

JAMES GREY

For Jeanette,

Greetings from York!

James

Prologue

The damp heat oozed around my body, wrapping itself around me like an oven's embrace. That clunky fan seemed to whirr in the distance somewhere across the hostel dormitory, but the old relic had evidently lost its fight against nature. I was only one-quarter conscious, but I could tell that the tropical sun had come up and begun baking the city into yet another fiery day. Not one breath of air brushed my skin.

My navy blue dress clung to me as I lay there, face down on the bottom bunk. My hands were tucked beneath the cheap, worn pillow that was mine for the week. I'd crept into my assigned bed late the night before. I'd been too lazy, too tipsy and far too careless to change into something more comfortable. Something a little less tight on the waist.

I was tossing and turning my way through that untamed land between sleep and wakefulness. Immersed in a dreamy denial that daylight was now flooding through the windows. But still, some distant part of me was aware that my hem had slid up. Right now I had my right knee bent and my left leg stretched out straight. Like some spider-superhero scaling a wall, only horizontal. The heat had made me do it.

Of course I shouldn't have gone to bed in a dress like that. It wasn't slutty, but it wasn't exactly knee-length either. *That thing is not designed for lying down in public*, my sleepy brain protested. But I could hardly hear its voice. Not through that soupy semi-consciousness.

The way I was positioned, the bottom of the fabric wasn't far south of where my butt turned to thigh. I could feel the material stretching taut there, especially on the right side. Where I'd pulled up my knee. That was the side of the bed that opened out to the room.

Usually I strung up my beloved green and orange sarong – the one I'd bought over in Madras – at the end of the bed for a modicum of privacy. You never knew who might be coming or going in a backpacker place. But had I remembered to hang it last night? It would have been a dark fumble. I wouldn't have wanted to wake the others. Even after a few beers, dormitory etiquette was usually second nature to me. I had a feeling I might have overlooked my makeshift curtain on this occasion.

Whatever. My head swirled. We were eight degrees north of the equator. Thirty degrees Celsius. This climate was relentless, but still it felt like it was very early. Too early to start reconstructing my evening. My exhausted body insisted it was the middle of the night, even as the brightness of a new day probed at my eyelids. I wasn't anywhere near ready to face it. I was still a sleepy, fuzzy-brained mush.

I groaned and turned my head to face the wall, splaying my fingers wide apart under the pillow. The mattress was thin and lumpy. I turned on my side for a few minutes. Hotter. Sweatier. My thighs stuck together. My upper arms and my torso and my breasts broiled against each other.

Too much tacky skin on tacky skin: I couldn't hold the position. I rolled back onto my stomach once more, spread my limbs out again. The Spiderman pose once more. That faint voice inside me whispered something about my modesty, but I brushed its nudges away like a sleeping dog tossing its head at a fly. Lying this way was the only thing that worked right now.

Sleep. Comfort. Cool. Air between my limbs. Nothing else mattered.

I drifted through the hazy syrup of hot morning slumber once more. That hemline was still tight on my thighs.

I dozed dreamily on. Five minutes, ten minutes, an hour? Then came the draft.

A cool and gentle breeze from somewhere behind me. Refreshing as a forest brook, it gurgled up from beyond my bare toes, gliding over my faraway heels and my comatose calf muscles. It came and went, regular as the breath of a sleeping child. Had someone moved the fan?

I felt my legs open wider, urging the light kiss of air deep inside my sticky garment.

Deeper than...oh, my...I could really *feel* that. Like a touch, present and immediate, almost as if...*oh shit!* I'd clearly found time to remove my underwear before collapsing into a coma last night. I hadn't gone out *sans* panties, I was sure of that. Yet here I was, bare where I really shouldn't have been.

I was definitely a little more awake now.

But *fuck* that felt good!

I splayed my left knee a little more. Was that a soft sigh I just let out?

Where was my shame? Had this city and this country and this climate taken it prisoner? Shouldn't I *do* something? Roll over at the very least? Oh, but that delicate breeze…

It was getting more intense. Or, at least, more vivid to me. Each and every waft was touching me intimately now. The first few had gotten no further than my knees. The next wave had only run out of steam halfway along the soft, hungry flesh of my inner thighs. Now the tiny gusts were hitting my pussy.

Each one still took its sweet, slow time to get there. It coursed a slow passage along my legs, like a lover's gentle hands. Then it unfurled through the taut navy archway my dress had drawn. And finally it fell square onto my inflamed vagina, landing like the kiss of a feather.

I was instantly wet. I could feel the elemental clash of air and liquid meeting. Down there at my centre, it was simultaneously cool and warm. I shuddered in my torpor, and my fingers clawed at the clammy sheet.

A soft whimper escaped my lungs. I didn't know how this was happening, but it was okay if I was half-asleep, right? What happens in the tropics, stays in the tropics. *Right?* I hooked my right ankle over the edge of the bed. My legs couldn't go much further apart than they were now.

And then I froze awake.

A new touch. Not just air, this time. The lightest of tugs at my hem. A finger — or a thumb, maybe? — sliding beneath its strained fabric. *What the…?*

I tensed as I realized that the breeze up my skirt hadn't come from the window or a fan. It had been human breath. The pursed, invasive exhalations of someone who'd been watching me at close quarters. Somebody who must have been aroused by that indecent hemline, and perhaps by a glimpse of my red pussy in the shadow of my wicked, creeping dress. Someone who was caressing my right buttock with a single digit now.

I had no idea if anybody else was in the room at this time. If there was, there was a good chance they were all still asleep. Was there an audience? Did my unknown morning visitor seriously think I was still asleep?

What would happen if I moved or cried out? *Will this be taken from me?*

I tried to stifle a moan as best I could. I hoped I was asleep. If that was the case, then I wasn't responsible. Nobody could say I had been...well, nobody could judge me. Only the waking can be judged.

Don't say a word, Laura. Stay quiet as a mouse.

The beautiful, gentle breaths kept drizzling up my dress like honey falling onto strawberries. Yes, it was definitely a thumb hooked in there; I could feel the fingers splaying gently across the other side of the material. Another thumb joined it, gripping the left hem just like I gripped the head of the mattress underneath the pillow. Where nobody could see my white knuckles.

Fuck, who could it be? The hipster, chain-smoking Japanese guy in the top bunk opposite? The Australian with the magnificent stubble who'd smiled at me yesterday evening before losing himself in his phone instead of heading out with the rest of us young travellers? Or someone I hadn't crossed paths with yet?

Or what about the German artist with the short-cropped hair, the loose-fitting dress and those gorgeous tattoos all over her brown-tanned back and calves? We'd barely spoken thus far, but I was sure I hadn't mistaken that fire in her eyes.

Maybe I didn't *want* to know. Maybe I just wanted to wonder.

The hands were becoming forceful now. They were shoving my dress up to my waist. The pressure of the fabric was suddenly gone from where it had been. Now the tightness lay on my hips, while below that it was deliciously free. My entire bottom half was now naked, open for anybody in the room to ogle.

But I was asleep still. That's what I would tell them.

The breathing between my legs suddenly stopped.

I stopped breathing. I waited.

The fingers of the hands on my behind curled into claws, the nails sinking calmly into the creamy flesh there. Gently they scratched their way down the backs of my thighs.

Not painful. But not to be argued with either.

They traced their way down my calves. I wondered if one of the hands would seek to straighten my left leg into a more natural position. But the right hand gripped my right ankle instead, pushing my right leg up to mirror my left. Now both legs were bent sideways at the knee, just like the elbow of both arms were. I was poised to swim like a frog.

And I could feel my pussy and my anus spread open like some perverted buffet on the bed.

Don't moan out loud, Laura. Hold yourself.

A weight and a creaking at the foot of the mattress.

Skin brushed the flesh of my inner thighs, pushing my frog's legs uncomfortably far apart. Solid skin, with a slight rasp to the touch. In that moment I knew these fingers belonged to a man. My intruder was male.

Then my pussy felt his touch. Decisive and bold this time, two fingers nuzzling my wet, sticky opening. I could hear the squelch as they explored me. It sounded unnaturally loud in my head, that noise. So did the guttural cry that followed. It echoed around the room like I was standing at the bottom of the Grand Canyon. My entire body began to shudder in response. And the spasms got wilder, harder, more violent. The tired old bed squawked in protest, like a chicken being strangled. And on it went, until the entire scene began to shake and shudder and I could take it no more.

Chapter I

Oh Jesus, no. No, no, no! Not again.

I could feel the convulsion in my leg. I could smell the sweat on my skin. I could hear the remnants of my last moan dying in the back of my throat. But I knew that my body's pleasure ride had slammed into its final moments.

I groaned as reality swarmed into my thoughts. Fuck, fuck and fuck again! I was in my own bedroom in New York City. Fourth-floor apartment. Autumn chill and honking taxi horns outside. And inside, my radio alarm clock reading the news headlines. It was five-thirty in the morning.

Another groan. No more than five seconds ago — or so it felt — I'd been moaning with anticipation in that fantastic dream. Half of me was still there in that dorm, waiting, my legs spread like an eager animal. Another thing that had never actually happened on my teenage backpacking trip through Thailand.

Oh, the carefree night out and the dormitory bunk bed and the tight blue dress had been real enough, all right. The insistent morning heat and the no-underwear thing too.

Those insane levels of arousal. My dreams were always real...up to a certain point.

Sometimes they went on and on and on. All the way. I'd wake up sweating, panting and shuddering on a Saturday or Sunday morning, the willing victim of another orgasmic reverie. George would smile and shake his head, as if it were the strangest thing.

But this morning's trip down the rabbit hole was the cruellest one I could remember. It happened like that now and then, though. Your dreamiest sleep happens right before you wake up — wasn't that what they said? And this time was doubly crazy, because I'd already woken up in the dream itself. It made my head hurt.

I could never get used to how sudden the switch of realities was at moments like this. You could be far, far away, in another world and another lifetime, and then goddamn by-election results on local radio would jolt you into a confused frazzle. I really needed to get one of those clever lights that woke you up gradually.

I wouldn't have minded being shaken awake (*really* awake) in such a way that took my dream to its logical conclusion. Not that this was very likely, imprisoned in our two-bedroom apartment as we were. I sure wasn't going to get a happy ending like that from George. I wasn't even sure why we slept in the same bed anymore. I guess it was just a pretence we'd kept up for the kids. And even after they'd left for college, it was easier just to leave things as they were in the master bedroom.

We'd started that family when I was twenty. Only a year and a half after Thailand. Insanity. But what a *great* idea it had seemed at the time. I never thought it through. That freedom had slipped away in the blink of an eye.

And now with the kids having fled the nest, was there a chance I could reclaim that liberty? Not a hope in hell. Now

I was the prisoner of a new tyranny. My keepers? A career and a mortgage.

I'd done well for myself. I was the main breadwinner in our household. In fact, the house was entirely in my name. George was a journalist, unlucky enough to find himself in a shrinking, shrivelling industry. A dying art. He was lucky to have a job at all still, but pay rises were always out of the question at the interior design magazine that kept him on the payroll as its Features Writer. And his salary had already been bad ten years ago.

None of that was any kind of problem in financial terms. I was bringing home more than enough bacon from my job at Kerstein, one of the world's largest shipping firms. I had to oversee the legal side of the huge deals that went down. Multi-billion dollar stuff. And my role was such that the top-level meetings couldn't actually go ahead without me.

But the thing was, I'd lost my life.

Alarm calls like this were the norm for me now. I was always in the office by seven and only occasionally home before nine. I'd become one of those awful people who just lived on coffee, shovelled down some nondescript, pre-packed salad at their desks at three in the afternoon and checked their emails on vacation. I could see how I must have looked, as clearly as a ship's captain sees a lighthouse beam on a clear night. But I just kept sailing on towards the rocks. I didn't know how to turn the old girl around.

The long hours went hand-in-hand with big responsibility. I'd been in the company for fifteen years — only the second employer I'd been with since Harriet was born — and now I was among the most senior women in a firm of several thousand people. We had fifteen offices around the country. Blah blah blah.

I was so good at being cynical like this as I lay in bed cursing my alarm clock, especially when pleasure like this morning's had been cut short. For a few short moments, I would feel ready to throw it all away and seize control of my life again. But then I'd get to the office, wade into the swamp of work, bog down in the next meaningless short-term crisis and forget all about myself.

Now I put my hand to my forehead: all the heat from my dream had curled up just there, like a combustion chamber to spark into life. I could feel that pulse still racing in my temples. My body was still tense from the slow erotic build in my dream. Aroused too, of course. I didn't want to open my eyes.

George would already be downstairs, getting coffee ready and probably making a start on some article or other. For him mornings were the most productive time. During the week, I always woke up with an empty space next to me in the bed.

As I gradually floated into wakefulness, I realized that today was Friday. I reached over and switched off the radio, which by now had moved onto the traffic report. The situation on the roads sounded catastrophic as always. I just wanted to be alone with my thoughts for just a moment.

I wondered if I could take a little me-time in the shower. My right hand was certainly capable of rubbing out that pent-up desire my dream had erected. But I knew there wasn't any point. The work-machine in the back of my head was already whirring. *Can I get to that email before my eight o'clock?*

Already the tropical hallucination and its heaving clouds of lust were slipping away. No, my time in the en-suite would be about getting clean, grooming the basics and airbrushing that frown line as best I could. My thoughts were slowly getting sucked into the whirlpool of another day.

I sat up in bed and swung my legs over the edge. They were still in shaky dream-mode and standing up on them took a moment to get right, but I dragged myself towards the bathroom. My eyes still felt like gravel pits, but the mohair carpet was soft and forgiving beneath my bare feet. I caught a glimpse of my outline in the full-length mirror.

Not everything had changed since the years of which I'd just been dreaming. Somehow, even after all this time, I still had a good tan. It had stuck with me like a close friend ever since I'd worked it up in Thailand, living the sunny dream just as any young woman escaping the northern USA for the first time would do. I guess my skin was somehow receptive to it — maybe that Italian blood from my grandmother. That hint of summer colour still paired nicely with my hair: dark brown but with a hint of auburn. I was even still wearing a dress of sorts — hah!

Nothing sexy about this one though. The tired-looking night-garment, now more grey than white after so many years of slumber, had three teddy bears on the front. They sat there on my B-cup breasts and gazed out at the world, with that unnervingly enquiring look teddy bears always have on their faces. Those three bears would probably have annoyed me if I'd been the one who had to see them.

 So no tight navy number. And the same practical panties I'd gone to bed with remained firmly wedged in between my inner thighs. This was real life, and I had a workday to get ready for.

Those teddy bears were right to look enquiring.

Chapter II

"Are you getting something for dinner, or shall I?"

George was settled at the kitchen table already, coffee poised next to his laptop and no clutter anywhere near his workspace. He sat upright in his angular pinewood chair, a model of excellent posture as usual. He looked over at me with a friendly, patient smile. His teeth were still full and white after all these years. When we'd met, they were the first thing I noticed. The first thing that had made me think about kissing his mouth.

"Urgh, I don't know," I muttered as I scratched around the coat rack for something that would look decent over the pantsuit I'd picked for today. "I've got a ton of meetings today, Cindy is on vacation and — "

"Laura," he interrupted, "are you really going to tell me how busy you are again? It was a simple question."

I hated that I did that. When had I become one of those people who turned every conversation into one about work problems? I was well aware of how much of a trial it had to be for other people. When I stopped and thought about it,

George had my sympathies. I just never stopped and thought about it. Not before opening my mouth.

"Sorry," I said, trying to slow down my brain for a second as I slipped my arms into a black, single-breasted coat. "It'd be great if you could get something. I'm looking forward to the weekend."

"I'm glad," he said, sitting back and taking a sip from his favourite cream earthenware mug. But when he glanced up at me, it was with the air of a man who knew better than to get too excited about the impending two-day break. He knew he'd catch me perusing the finer details of a contract at some point.

"See you later," I said, trying to muster a tone somewhere between hopeful and promising — even though I knew better than to hope or promise. I walked over to where my husband was sitting and kissed him on the greying stubble that covered his cheek.

I liked how he smelled of soap and shampoo at this time in the early morning. If only—

I had to go.

Six minutes later I was hurtling along in the subway, thinking *maybe I'm the problem.*

It must have been over six months since George and I had had anything even approaching sex. I had always thought it was something that happened to other people, that fire in the bedroom fizzling out. But our droughts had been getting longer and longer, and this one was a record-breaker. Could it be that we were done for good?

But then there was the awkward fact that my libido had been steadily on the rise in the five years since I'd turned forty. So if we weren't having sex, then, it had to be because George didn't want it. Maybe it was because he was eight years older than me and didn't care any more. I supposed he'd started dreaming of young and beautiful college girls by now. Who knew what went on in a middle-aged guy's head? I probably didn't *want* to know. I certainly hadn't dared to ask.

When you marry way too young, and for all the wrong reasons, talking things out can fall by the wayside. It turns into a chess game. You spend your time trying to guess what's in the other person's mind. Why did they *do* that? That line...was it code for something? What does this silence mean? That's what happened with us, anyway. We only said the harmless stuff out loud.

One part of me was fixed on that idea that he wanted a pretty young thing and that I was no longer that girl. At least, not when I looked in the mirror. I saw a plump little whale with shapeless hips and that frown line that drove me crazy. That careless youngster in the navy blue dress had left the stage for good.

So that was all there was to it. George aged very gracefully and I was more than happy to still have sex with him, but I was sure he didn't want it. There you had it — the problem was on his side. Well, apart from the fact that I was obviously a whale.

But as the subway car ploughed its way through New York's guts like some giant, rattling mole on steroids, suddenly I wondered if it was all that simple. When he interrupted me this morning, there'd been a particular look on his face. One that I couldn't get out of my mind. It wasn't the exasperation I might have expected. More than anything else, his face had spoken of defeat.

Had *I* made him give up on me? Worn him down and turned him off by making everything about work? Now that I thought about it, I'd probably started every evening in that six-month famine with a lengthy declaration of how mad, stressed and tired I was after a long day. I'd taken calls at dinner. Complained about Andre. What part of any of that would make him think I might have had getting pounded on the sturdy dining-room table in mind?

And as for those weekend dreams that ran the full course, well, I was done when I woke up, wasn't I? He'd be thinking he was surplus to requirements, wouldn't he? Now that I considered it, I guess me dreaming about God-knew-who doing God-knew-what to me couldn't have been any more empowering a thought for him than the idea of him ogling 22-year-old blondes was for me.

How had I been so blind?! George had never been the grab-you-by-the-hair and drag you to the bedroom kind of guy. He was more empathetic than egotistical. He only woke up when you showed him you wanted it. *Shit, Laura, you always initiated sex! YOU'RE the one who stopped!*

I shook my head, stunned by the breakthrough I'd just made. The simplicity of it! I'd been so caught up in thinking of reasons why George didn't want to sleep with me and wasn't interested in me, I'd forgotten to show him I still wanted it. When was the last time I had dropped a hint, made an approach, worn something sexy? Who flicked the switch on that stuff?

Probably it was to do with work. It had just happened. There's no way I would consciously have decided to stop communicating my urges to my husband. Hell no — they were there all the time! Well, I probably let them get buried by life, but that was just a thing that happened. If anyone had asked, they'd have found my hot desires weren't hidden very deep at all.

Right now they were pushing at the trapdoor, trying everything they could to get out. I couldn't shake this sudden fantasy that I was back home in the bedroom and slipping on my silkiest lingerie. It made me press my legs together. I sat upright, took a sharp breath and rolled my tongue across my upper front teeth. I'd always done that when I was aroused.

Now a plan began to form in my mind. I looked around the lurching underground carriage. Eyes on phones, fingers flicking through magazines and the occasional blank stare into space. Nobody blinked. Who else could be thinking about sex at this time in the morning? No suspicious smirks at all. Just stony faces. Did *mine* tell a story?

My mind was getting carried away with scenarios. I'd forgotten just how nice it could be for such a reverie to take me during the daytime. It always felt a good kind of naughty to be in a public place with thoughts like that churning around in my imagination.

So good, in fact, that I ended up missing my subway stop.

Which meant I did not, in fact, get to that email before the 8am meeting. In fact, I was seven minutes late for that 8am. I never did that.

This, of course, did not escape the attention of my colleague Andre.

"Most unlike you, Laura," he taunted before I'd even had a chance to dump my laptop bag and my coat on the glass table in the conference room. "You know we've got a deadline on this deal, right? Maybe you want to wind that alarm clock a bit earlier next time?"

That was Andre for you. Total dick. And one with a knack for making a reference that could make you blush. How did he know to bring up the subject of this morning's wake-up call?

I just glared at him. He wasn't even my boss. We were in fact equals, working together on what would hopefully be the biggest cargo deal our company had ever concluded. He was the negotiations guy; I was the voice of legal reason.

"Good morning, Daniel. Good morning, Mark." I smiled to the other people gathered in the room, turning deliberately away from Andre. We were meeting with our prospective clients from Britain, as we always did at this time on a Friday. We'd been sitting around tables like this for several weeks already, so we knew each other well, but still I couldn't let Andre's jerkish comments escalate.

"Hi Laura!" said the guys from Danscombe, the heavyweight manufacturing company we hoped to work with. Nice men, both thoroughly English in a cheerful, cheeky-schoolboy sort of way. "Happy Friday!"

Why couldn't Andre be like them? The answer, probably, apart from his being a natural bully, was that he was extraordinarily hot. Brought up in Los Angeles, he'd obviously been able to say whatever he wanted his whole life, and still have women dropping at his feet.

He was thick-set and sturdy, but almost six feet tall. A touch of Latino blood added an alluring darkness to his sharp features. His grey-green eyes stabbed you something fierce if they fixed on yours from beneath his heavy brow. His dark-brown hair had a hint of explosive curl about it, but he kept it cropped close and tight. And he wore a five o'clock shadow at all times.

Andre had a penchant for blue suits, and could pull them off in any shade he pleased. I'd watched women strain (and fail) to avert their eyes when he turned to the window to consider a proposition while gazing at the city skyline. He knew exactly what he was doing when he placed his hands on the hip-high metal bar that ran in front of the floor-to-ceiling glass, bending over ever so slightly at the waist as he steadied himself over the city.

This stuff mattered in our line of work. We'd already witnessed an early change in personnel where our counterparts at Danscombe were concerned. Initially their negotiator had been a certain Nicole, but now Daniel had the job — and I strongly suspected that the substitution had been down to Andre's quite stunning effect on the opposite sex. The tall, beer-loving brunette totally knew her stuff on paper, but she'd gone twinkle-eyed when put in a room with Andre. In the second week of talks she'd absent-mindedly conceded to him on a point that would have cost their company millions had my legal opposite number Mark not stepped in to correct her. We didn't see Nicole again after that day.

From a business point of view, the Board appreciated all of these advantages Andre brought to the table. It wasn't just the superficial stuff that he could exploit. He was annoyingly smart, quick-witted and artful. In short, he was disturbingly good at what he did. Everyone at Kerstein knew that, which is why I was stuck with him.

There was no way we weren't going to be working together on high-level contracts like the one with Danscombe. Andre was the firm's top deal-maker by miles. I was without question the most qualified and experienced legal brain. It had to be this way. Nobody said we had to be friends.

And that was absolutely never going to happen. I won't lie and say I didn't stop and gulp the first time I saw him, just the same as every other woman did, but from the moment he opened his mouth I couldn't stand the guy. Meeting Andre in a bar might have been one thing. Passing him and his cologne in the hallway certainly had an effect. But if you really knew him, or had the misfortune to work with him, then you knew he was just unpleasant.

Not like Daniel and Mark. They might have been across a high-stakes negotiating table from us, but they were still decent human beings.

"Happy Friday!" I said to the Englishmen. It had become a bit of a tradition for us to say something along those lines to each other. While Andre never liked to show any sign of weakness, I didn't see the harm in sharing the odd smile with the Danscombe guys.

"All right, so it's almost the weekend," he said sarcastically, gesturing at my chair. "When you're finished dreaming about your Sunday picnic, maybe we can begin?"

That was typical Andre. Even if he couldn't be directly rude to the clients, he could take an indirect poke at them through me. And the more power he showed over *me*, the more power he exuded in the room generally. Not that I thought any of that was necessarily a conscious strategy on his part. It just came naturally to him.

Andre loved himself to a sickening degree. My policy was to ignore him as much as possible, at least when we were in front of other people. Working with him on a regular basis had been chipping away at my soul for nearly four years now. I couldn't wait for this particular negotiation to be over. Legally speaking, I had reason to hope that it might not be much longer.

"So, I went through the latest proposed contract last night," I said, putting my policy into action. "And from Kerstein's point of view I think we could be ready to formalize matters. From my side there aren't any outstanding discussion points and it's just paperwork from here onwards."

Andre snorted.

"Oh, er...you didn't see my email from last night?" enquired Daniel. He sounded really awkward.

I sighed a little sigh to myself. *That* email.

"I have to admit I didn't," I confessed. "Not just yet."

Just as I did every day of my working life, I wondered how I'd stumbled into a world where you were expected to write and read emails in the dead of night or at the crack of dawn. But I had become good at that world. Usually I would have been up to speed ahead of this session. I'd have skimmed my inbox on the subway. But today had not been a usual sort of a day so far.

"No matter, I saw it," Andre interjected impatiently, throwing a dark glance my way. "It seems we've got a lot more talking to do still, don't we gentlemen?"

I could feel the heat rising in the room. After several days in which the talks had moved in the direction of agreement, something serious was clearly going down.

Mark spoke first: "To fill you in, Laura, our London headquarters have pushed back on the delivery time expectations. We cannot go ahead on the basis of a 19-day voyage from Singapore to Sydney, for example. Nor can Shanghai to Los Angeles be allowed to take 27 days. It's too long a delay for our sales cycle."

Andre leaned over the table like a confident bull poised to charge a matador. His arms were locked crowbar-straight; his knuckles were a bloodless white on the glass.

"You are well aware of how much time we need to allow for adverse weather conditions and other delays! This is just a worst-case-scenario clause!"

I knew better. It was a clause that allowed us the flexibility to pick up and drop off cargo in other ports along the way, maximizing our profits for the journey. But I held my tongue.

"Maybe so," said Daniel, with the air of someone who knew exactly what I knew. "But we cannot take your word on that. As it stands, Kerstein can use all of that time on every trip with no penalty."

He was dead right with that. Clearly somebody over in London had been doing their homework.

"We have to protect ourselves against potential litigation," I chimed in. "It's standard procedure to err on the safe side with our promises."

"Not where we come from," said my counterpart Mark. "Under-promising and over-delivering doesn't work in this game. We're not looking for pleasant surprises here. We want realistic terms."

He didn't add the words 'or we'll take our money elsewhere,' but we could all feel the unsaid line ringing in our ears.

I wasn't going to get much more involved in the conversation. I was there for black-and-white legal stuff, not this kind of dialogue. We were entitled to push for whatever terms we felt were right for us, but we certainly weren't laying our cards on the table as honestly as we might have done. This particular issue was a grey area at best. Like a big, grey elephant in the room. I wasn't comfortable with it, and I let Andre do the talking. He'd be like a dog with a bone — and I knew he'd run with it.

The conversation went back and forth for several minutes. And the longer it went on, the more serious the atmosphere grew. Andre kept on repeating that the delivery deadlines were simply a case of us being conservative. The Danscombe team saying — without actually saying it — that they weren't going to fall for that one. Until finally somebody started talking numbers.

"We want a 25% reduction in your delivery deadlines," said Daniel in an even tone. "We know these journeys can be executed significantly faster. And if this deal goes through, more than half the cargo on every one of your ships will be ours. Our interests should therefore take priority."

"How about 10%?" said Andre. "And we sign the contract today."

I choked back a snort of my own. We both knew the papers would take far longer than that to finalize. But Andre knew that empty words were often enough to change the course of history.

Daniel hesitated. I sensed both of them wanted to get home after so many weeks of living in a Manhattan hotel room. Danscombe only flew them home one weekend in three, and that was hardly worth doing. I knew they were exhausted by these negotiations — we all were — and I could tell he was tempted. Even if you were buying shoes, 10% always sounded like a discount worth having. And until now, this pair had been pretty easy to convince on most points. And this was time — not money.

But today the vibe was different. Mark spoke once more, sounding more serious than I could ever remember him sounding. "Dan, we're going to talk to the office on this one. We have very clear instructions. Everyone, let's reconvene next week."

Even Andre was stunned into silence.

Chapter III

I didn't bring my work home with me that night.

Things hadn't gone to plan at the office, but for once I wasn't much concerned about that. I had a plan of my own for the evening and it couldn't fail. I was buzzing with a particular kind of excitement I hadn't felt for the longest time. I got home at six-thirty, which qualified as an early getaway these days, even for a Friday night. My heart thudded as I put the key into the front door.

As the cool, jagged metal slipped into the slot and the latch gave way to a light twist of my fingers, I couldn't help thinking I might be unlocking my sex life again. I'd thought that particular door had been slammed in my face forever — until my morning epiphany. This was going to be as good as one of my dreams. Better, actually, because I fully intended to see it through.

I'd been toying with scenarios all day. Most of them had degenerated into the sort of things that happened in my head when I was asleep. Deeds beyond the basics of intercourse. Possibilities I'd suppressed somewhere deep inside since I'd turned into a working adult. Things I'd never have the confidence to try out in reality — not any more, at least. Things I daren't even tell you.

None of these were quite appropriate for a first foray back into intimacy. George hadn't ever been a man to push me out of my sexual comfort zone, not even back when we were fucking on a regular basis. He wasn't selfish or anything, just not much of a leader in the bedroom. Neither of us was. So my fantasies had been buried since my backpacking days. Still, sex had always been fun enough whenever we'd had it.

No, I definitely didn't need anything fancy tonight. After all this time living like a nun, plain old missionary position would seem like a Kamasutra move. I just wanted to feel wanted. Tonight was all about the seduction.

And I was sure that part would be easy. Now that I'd allowed myself to believe that George might still have some lust to his name and a wish to use his dick on me, all I had to do was invite him in. I just had to be loud and clear about it.

A pleasant, meaty smell greeted me as I closed the door with the soft click behind me. I could hear a sizzle coming from the kitchen too. Hmm. Something porky, that was my guess. George had always been a substantially better cook than I was, and suddenly I realized I'd skipped eating all day again. Even if today, for once, it was my drifts into fantasy rather than work that had made me do it.

"Hey, I'm home," I called out above the hiss of what I was really starting to hope were sausages. I could hardly recognize my own voice. It sounded upbeat and chirpy for a change. This time I hadn't brought home my usual end-of-week defeat, unfinished business and exhaustion.

"Ah, you're quite early," replied George's voice. "Did they lock you out of the office or something?"

"Nothing like that," I answered carefully, throwing my scarf and my coat over the back of the sofa. "I've got a few other things I need to take care of, real soon. Stuff that's been on my mind today."

I couldn't see him yet. He was just out of sight around the kitchen door. I could feel anticipation coiling up tighter in my gut as I said those last words.

"Well, since you're here, maybe I don't need to keep your dinner warm for later after all. I just need to finish the gravy and we could eat soon. Will you be ready to sit down in 10 minutes?"

He hadn't detected the flirty purr in my voice at all. Well, why would he? I hadn't done that kind of talk in months. During which time he'd probably mastered the art of tuning me out. Especially when I'd just clattered in from work, a raging bundle of keys and laptop bags and coats and problems.

But there was no hurry. He'd get the message soon enough. A few minutes were all I needed.

"Sounds good. I'll just freshen up in the bedroom and be right back."

"Great."

We weren't a garrulous couple these days. But there was no sarcasm, no animosity, no silent loathing in the way we talked to each other. We just didn't do automatic kisses or 'darlings' or unnecessary sugarcoating. It hadn't seemed right for a long while now.

But tomorrow morning, maybe it *would* seem right. I hoped so, because things were going to change around here, starting tonight. I smiled a wicked little smile and straightened out that slouch in my back as I walked up the stairs. Oh yes, tonight was going to be good.

I'd considered stripping off, going down the stairs naked and tiptoeing into the kitchen doorway. I'd wait there until he looked up from stirring the gravy and noticed me. He'd do a double-take, of course — and then the inevitable would happen.

But since my belly was now rumbling almost as insistently as my pussy was aching, I ditched that idea. Showing up so dramatically after such a long time might give poor George a heart attack, anyway. No, we could eat first. The inevitable could occur after dinner...what was another half an hour after this long a wait?

Anyway, I figured it might be fun if I let things happen slowly. Reveal my intentions to him with micro-moves.

Upstairs in the bedroom, I made straight for the closet. I pulled out the perfect thing for an unrushed, subtle sort of surprise. It was a sheer white button-up blouse that I probably hadn't worn for about three years. It was nothing suggestive or slutty, but a touch too tight for work. I think the last time I'd been anywhere in it was nothing more exciting than Saturday morning shopping with a couple of girlfriends. For tonight, though, it was ideal. The kind of garment that could sneak up on a guy.

I laid the blouse out on the bed, which as usual George had made during the course of the day. I wondered if the inevitable would happen right here where the crisp blouse lay waiting, or somewhere downstairs. I'd been thinking all day about that dining room table, and how little use it got. Nowadays we ate all our meals in the kitchen and never had anybody over. But it was a solid old thing, passed down from George's grandparents. The kind of furniture they don't make anymore. Furniture that could take a person's weight in its stride, should the need arise.

My mind was running wild again.

Come on Laura, focus on getting dressed now!

Trying to focus, I shook off my modest kitten heel shoes and slipped the business pants down my legs. I walked over to the chest of drawers in just the dull panties and the shirt I'd worn at work. Even *that* felt naughty: God, I was in desperate need!

I pulled the second drawer halfway out and rummaged at the very back with my right hand. I didn't need to use my eyes, because the thing I sought was going to feel very different from the rest of my underwear. When my fingers closed on a light wisp of fabric, coarse to the touch as I drew my thumb across the material, I knew I had what I wanted.

Quickly I changed my panties, feeling strange and exposed in that long-lost lingerie. Then I pulled off my shirt and unclipped my bra. Naked but for the wispy number I could barely feel on my waist, I diligently gathered up everything I'd taken off and trotted it over to the washing basket in the bathroom. I didn't want mess strewn all over the bed if we ended up coming in here. Not those miserable work things, anyway.

My nipples were hardening already, not just from the thrill of choosing a devious outfit but from the chill in the air. It was deep into October, but not quite wintery enough for us to have put the central heating on yet. We were in that in-between zone. For other couples, it would have been prime cuddling season.

Well, it wouldn't hurt if my tits showed through the button-up blouse. I hastily pulled it on. Sure was tight, but it meant I could go braless. I knew my breasts would show their shape in this.

And how to complete the outfit? Walking in wearing a short skirt would be almost as obvious as appearing in the kitchen totally naked. But jogging pants were too far in the other direction. I needed something along the lines of the tight, white blouse: sexy if you wanted it to be.

Jeans crossed my mind, but the whole thing would make me look like some cartoon cowgirl. So I settled on close-fitting ankle pants, black with a starry night pattern. Not garishly tight across the butt, but with enough of a stretch to bring out a curve or two. The casual observer — or someone who didn't quite know what the evening held in store yet — could buy the line that I'd chosen these for comfort.

I'd grown used to the idea that George wasn't really much of an observer at all, but I figured even *he* might ask questions of high heels when all I ever did at the end of the week was kick off my shoes as quickly as possible. So I pulled on a pair of black socks, quickly dabbed on some not-too-obvious make-up in the bathroom and took a moment in front of the mirror.

I was glad to be fundamentally good-looking. I probably made it hard for my face to look its best, what with all that worrying and rushing around from meeting to meeting. I often caught myself forgetting to breathe during the day, which I was pretty sure wasn't all that good for my skin. Thank God, then, that nature had given me some stubbornly good fundamentals.

I had full lips and healthy, rounded cheeks. They occupied a pleasantly curving face that sat in the good range: neither overly plump nor long, thin and mean. My chin swooped nicely — I would have hated an angular jut. I had blue-green eyes that could still sparkle when they wanted to. Neat, shapely teeth that I never thought twice about showing should the need to smile arise. A little sharpness to my nose and my eartips, which could at once be both cute and not-to-be-messed-with. Lawyers need that last part.

Sure, my hair wasn't perfect. If anything betrayed my lifestyle, it was the slight panic each strand seemed to have suffered at the ends. I liked the colour, but there was a frizzy volume to my shoulder-length ponytail that probably needed some attention. Maybe I would do something about it on the weekend. Now, I just gave it a quick smooth-over, re-tied it and went downstairs.

Dinner smelled even better than before. I crossed the darkened living room with a thudding heart, anxious from the burden of trying to act normal when clearly nothing was.

I could have sworn the intent in every footstep rang out so loud and clear that George would come to investigate, spoiling my slow build.

But if there was anything obviously unusual about me or my behaviour, my husband gave no sign that he had picked up on it as I walked in. He was busy dishing food onto the plates — sausages, I guessed right! — and didn't even look up.

He was bracing himself for my end-of-week rant, most likely. Well, he was going to get a pleasant surprise tonight.

"I'm *so* glad we're having sausages! I'm starved! I didn't manage to — I mean, well, I'm just starved!"

"Me too," he said, ladling the last of the gravy over the meat, mashed potatoes, peas and carrots. "And your timing's good. I'm all done!"

"Thanks George, I'll take these over to the table."

"Just going to wash my hands quickly."

I sat down with a smile on my lips, watching him from behind as he disappeared towards the small bathroom at the far end of the kitchen. The jeans *he* wore definitely worked for me right now. He wore blue denim almost every day, and every pair of pants he owned hugged his hips like cling-wrap. I don't think George had ever set foot inside a gym, but he still had the same trim figure as the day I married him. How had this ever been difficult?

It was only when he emerged from the bathroom and walked back towards our little square kitchen table that he actually laid eyes on me for the first time that evening. I noticed his gaze drop from my face to my blouse and back to my lightly made-up face again.

"You look different," he said quietly, taking his place and tucking straight into the food.

"Do I?" I replied with a casual shrug. "Is that a good thing?"

He cocked his head to the side as he shovelled a pile of peas onto his fork. "Well it's nothing bad, not at all. I just can't place it, exactly."

"Well, life is full of mystery," I said as I got going on my piping-hot meal. "So anyway, how was your day?"

He gave me a funny look. I felt guilty for the fact that he wasn't used to that question. My job had made me a monstrous wife!

"Er, pretty good, actually," he said cautiously. "I had a nice flow going on the writing today. I was thinking of doing a book on the side, actually. I've been chewing over some ideas."

"That sounds like a smart move. Diversify your portfolio and put some eggs in another basket. But before you tell me more about it, I'm getting a glass of wine. Want to join me?"

Normally George wasn't much of a drinker, but on this occasion he nodded with a smile. It felt like he was dropping his guard already. I liked the way the vibe in the room was going.

I went to the fridge, brought a bottle of Chardonnay to the kitchen counter and poured out a glass for each of us. Before turning back to face him, I reached up to my blouse with one hand and quickly undid the uppermost button.

I wasn't even into cleavage territory yet, but it was a start. My little seduction was ever so slightly under way.

Halfway through dinner, while George checked a message on his phone, I let another button go. This time he noticed the adjustment.

"You seem very relaxed tonight, Laura," he remarked with a quick glance at the new expanse of exposed skin beneath my collarbone. He was a little awkward about it, but I couldn't blame him for treading carefully after so long.

You might have to tone down the subtlety soon…

"Oh, I'm just happy it's the weekend," I smiled, allowing myself a good stretch that tightened the blouse across my chest almost to popping point. "I want to really enjoy it for once, you know?"

He coughed and gave me a funny look. Was he starting to get on my wavelength?

When he agreed to a refill on the wine, I came back with a third button undone. And I knew the inevitable was close.

George stayed cool, saying nothing, rising to the challenge. His suspiciousness was seeping away, and it felt like we'd gone back in time. I was enjoying this.

We finished every last scrap on our plates. We were close to draining our second glasses of wine by that stage. And George was visibly more relaxed. He was looking in my direction a lot more than usual, no question about that. He hardly touched his phone.

"I'm stuffed, George," I said, leaning back in my chair with a satisfied sigh and the remnants of Chardonnay number two in my right hand. "You've outdone yourself."

"Oh, I thought that was a pretty regular dinner, but thanks," he answered.

I countered by raising my left hand and flicking another button-hold apart. I could feel that my nipples were on the verge of escape. This time I held his gaze.

And he held mine.

I could feel the excitement humming between us now.

Has it really been this easy all along?

"You want another one?"

"Another Chardonnay, you mean?" he asked with a twinkle in his eye. Oh, the tease! "Why yes, I believe I will..."

Fine, we could still play a slow game.

By the time he came back with a third glass for each of us, I was down to my last three buttons. My firm breasts were free.

He sat down but didn't lean back. Bolt upright, he placed his hands on his thighs, splaying his knees. He let his eyes rove down my chest, then back up to my eyes again.

"What is it?" I enquired, an exaggeratedly innocent look on my face.

He chuckled. "Oh, nothing. You just really *are* very relaxed tonight, it seems."

"Maybe a little," I grinned. "So, you really want to finish that wine or—?"

His reply was to reach across the table and undo my remaining blouse buttons. His face wore a look that I hadn't seen for a long time, but which I liked very much.

I wriggled out of my blouse, flicking it away onto the floor as I got the sleeve off my left wrist. Topless at the kitchen table I may have been, but I felt confident and in control. Plus, I had an idea.

"How about going and sitting on that kitchen counter over there? I'll do something nice for you. Not cooking, I promise!"

He stood up, holding my gaze. I couldn't help noticing a clear bulge in those jeans of his. He took the three paces over to our worktop and hoisted himself onto it. Behind him were the big jars containing wooden spoons, potato mashers, that kind of thing. Above his head, the shelf full of cookbooks. Next to him, the stove.

I followed George across the room, and stood facing him. For the first time in as long as I could remember, I stripped naked in front of my husband. It wasn't elegant, but it sure was a torrent of adrenaline. I kept licking my lips in anticipation, while the swelling grew bigger each time my eyes darted down to his crotch.

I grabbed another swig of wine from the table before stepping right up to him and undoing yet another button. This time, it was the one on the front of his jeans.

"Lean back, if you can," I suggested.

He propped his hands flat on the countertop and rocked back, giving me space to unzip him, reach behind the stretch of his boxers and pull out his stiff cock with my right hand.

I didn't want to start off with slow licks along his shaft, gradually building him up. Tonight, I wanted to wow him with fireworks.

So I bent my waist, pushed my hair out of the way, crammed as much of his dick into my mouth as I could, and got to work.

He was groaning right away.

Well, he'd been deprived for a long time.

I felt like such a good wife, gulping down on his shaft as it threatened to explode right onto my throat.

I added my own moans to the chorus, gagging and salivating and greedily gobbling his taste all at the same time. Everything was *so right*. How had it ever been wrong?

"Ugh...uhhh...you better stop, Laura, you're going to make me come already…"

I popped my lips off him like I'd never been away. "A shame, I could go all night!" I cooed, straightening up and putting my hands on either side of his hips. "Although I do want *that* between my legs," I added hastily.

"Uh, yes," he replied with a glazed look on his face.

"I had another idea for that…"

Everything was going so well, after all. Why not push for the perfect finish?

I leaned forward and whispered in his ear.

"It's time we really *used* that dining room table."

"Hmm," he murmured. "That sounds like a fun idea."

"Follow me then!" I said as I spun around on my heels and marched towards the door leading into the living room. I was light-headed now. Walking on air. I could do anything I wanted.

The big old table was the first thing on your right as you emerged from the kitchen, taking up a whole corner of the room next to the flight of stairs leading up to the bedroom. The dining table was just above waist-height for me, and I hopped aboard with ease.

The rough oak wood was cold on my skin, but every bit as delightfully coarse on my back as I knew it would be. I'd run my hands along it enough dreamy times in the past to have certain expectations. I nestled down, pressing my shoulder blades into the hard, gnarly wood, drawing my knees up high towards me so my heels were poised on the very edge of the table. I placed my hands on my breasts, enjoying the way they cupped them, my palms lightly caressing my nipples, as I waited.

George took ten or twenty seconds to follow me through the door. For a moment, my fears and doubts flashed before my eyes. My heart began to beat harder as I wondered where he was. But no, he'd just been pulling off those tight jeans of his. And now he was there, smiling at me between my parted knees.

"How about I taste you?" he grinned. "I forgot to make dessert."

"Oh, help yourself!"

My back arched off the table in delight the moment I felt the first touch of his tongue down there. I squeezed my breasts hard with my nails as his mouth began to rove all the way up and down my pussy. He was savouring my wetness and my taste for himself, and the very fact he was doing so was almost enough to make me come right there, moments after he'd started. After so many months of neglect, the intensity of touch was like ice and fire all at once. It was almost too much.

My mind flashed back to the unfinished business of that morning's dream. This was how it was meant to end! The stranger who'd dared to exploit my carelessness had turned out to be a trusted lover. One who had flipped me over, spread my legs and begun to lick me out. I did not have to be outraged. I was free to let go.

And let go I did. Right there on the dining room table. Spasm after spasm ran through my body as I exploded almost embarrassingly fast. I'd been so fucking horny, wound up by months of deprivation and one very hot dream. And I knew there was more to come as George replaced his mouth with his cock.

If his tongue down there had been exquisite, then I don't know what word could describe the feeling of him sliding inside me for the first time in so long. I didn't care either — I just clutched the edge of the table in my curled fingers and revelled. The hardness beneath me and the hardness within me.

George thrust gently at first, but it was only a few moments before that turned into a primal, rhythmic pounding. Neither of us wanted to hang around, and once he quickened he went harder than usual. It hurt a little to feel him after so long, but definitely not in a bad way. He came quickly, of course, and his grunts had hardly subsided when I climaxed for a second time in two minutes. It was a moment before I stopped seeing stars.

"Fuck, George," I panted as he twitched his last seed inside me, a deep satisfaction written all over his face. "We should do that more often."

"I think you're right," he smiled. "That's how you really start a weekend."

He leaned forward, resting his weight on his hands as he placed them on the table, and kissed me. Full on the mouth, his tongue curling gently behind my top lip. I grappled to drink in as much of the kiss as I could. I had forgotten how good it was to join our mouths like that.

Just one more thing we needed to do more often.

Chapter IV

But I had gotten it wrong with George. Big time. Spectacularly and monumentally wrong. There was no new beginning. Far from it.

Turned out my misreading of the situation was nothing of the sort. Turned out I hadn't actually been paying enough attention to the situation at all. Turned out I hadn't given my instincts nearly enough credit.

And it turned out that sexy dinner date — the one that was going to put us back on the rails — was exactly the thing that pushed the truth out of my husband.

When the dust had settled the following morning, when the cuddling was over and the wake-up sex didn't happen and something didn't feel quite right over breakfast, George finally sat me down at that same kitchen table and told me he had something to say to me.

He hadn't ever used that phrase. But I knew what those words meant. I'd watched enough movies in my time to understand what would come. I could almost see the confession forming on his lips, every gory syllable of it, before it actually tumbled out of his mouth.

"Laura, I'm seeing somebody else."

He couldn't even look me in the eye as he said it.

And immediately I felt nauseous. I was sick at my own stupidity. I breathed harder and deeper and stared at the wall behind his left shoulder, but I didn't want to yell or throw anything. My only emotion was that I was the dupe for even *thinking* this was ever about me. That I'd been the worst kind of fool the night before. I had to get out of the room. Away from these ugly truths.

"Wait, Laura…"

He didn't even sound like he wanted me to wait. Somehow that added the first sledgehammer-blow of hurt to the cocktail. My eyes welled with tears as I abandoned the last cup of coffee George would ever make for me.

The divorce was through in three months. Let's just say there are some advantages to having legal skills.

As for the day-to-day stuff, George was out of the house by the following weekend. He didn't even try to argue that he should hang around. I got the feeling that all the gutless coward had needed was a push to tell me what was up and move on with his life.

George had always needed those little nudges. And on this occasion it was nothing other than my lust-fuelled evening that had guilted him into fessing up. How vicious the irony was.

It stung like crazy. Maybe we'd been drifting, but marriage is one heck of an investment to come crashing down in one sentence. Only the death of a loved one could make you feel loss harder in one hit, surely? But still, I had to be thankful I'd gotten a bee in my bonnet that night. Who knows how long it would have taken for his treachery to come out?

I don't know why I had to know the details. But I did.

My intuition that he wanted some pretty young thing more than me? Spot-on. Of course she was a twenty-something. A clueless 24-year-old brunette from Vermont, to be precise. She was in her first city job, a junior post at a marketing agency. One of her assignments happened to have involved calling up George on behalf of a client offering its living room suite to be featured in a photo shoot. That was how they'd met. Classic journalist-and-PR-girl. She'd probably fallen right into his lap.

What George could give her, other than a father-figure vibe with salt-and-pepper facial hair, amounted to just about nothing. He wasn't even rich — as the divorce terms had by now firmly reminded him. If she'd grown used to any sugar linked to *my* bank account, well, life was going to get a lot less sweet from now on.

Still, we all make dumb mistakes when we're young. I knew that better than anybody. She would learn soon enough that she was barking up a withering tree.

I'd never understood why people felt culpable after being cheated on by a significant other, but now that it had happened to me, it all made perfect sense. It would have been far easier if the lava pit of anger inside me was the only thing I had to deal with. But no, that same sense of guilt that had driven me to seduce him that Friday night still stalked me now — only it was ten times more intense. Had *I* been the one to send him into the arms of another? A girl who no doubt rode him hard at every opportunity, earned even less than he did, wore shiny clothes and never bothered him with office talk?

I tried to piece together the timeline in my mind: did he first hook up with her before or after our sex life started to wane? He was vague about when exactly they'd met, and would go no further than saying it had been 'a few months'. But I suspected he might have been rounding that down. And

I couldn't place an exact date on our own decline either. Things die gradually; the memory plays tricks.

You beat yourself up about all the signs you missed, too. The sex was one thing. There I was, thinking it was just because his thoughts were drifting to some glowing young hottie. It had never crossed my unforgivably innocent mind that he might actually be *acting* on those fantasies. And shouldn't I have smelled her on his skin? Or questioned the times he didn't look me in the eye when we spoke about his plans for the day?

Of course I felt like an utter fool. Furious, yes, but disgraced and responsible too. Not so much for being played like a puppet, but for having my time wasted like that. Especially in what I knew, deep down, was actually supposed to be the prime of my life.

Sadly, I responded to my new-found freedom in the only way I knew how. I hurled myself even deeper into the abyss of my job. Why come home at nine when I could come home at eleven? There was always a little more fine print to read. All those tiny words were way better than an empty house.

It wasn't a case of missing George. That would have been even more stupid. He was a cheat, and we hadn't had much of a relationship by the end anyway. I wasn't missing *him*, no. I just didn't appreciate the hole he left: the reminder that I was no longer wanted. And of what an idiot I'd been. Not just in failing to spot that something as big as that could have been going on, but for getting in my own way so much. For letting my own life get so one-dimensional.

And yet here I was, knowingly letting it get even worse. Workplace escapism of the unhealthiest kind. It helped me get through the darkest months of winter, but when the first signs of spring began to show in late March, I was still waist-deep in the idea that none of this mattered, because I didn't have time for a relationship anyway. Part of me had wanted out for years, so what was the problem, really?

And sex had disappeared from my life well before the divorce, anyway, so I'd lost nothing at all there. Right?

I knew this rationalizing wasn't healthy for so many reasons. But I kept on doing it. There was plenty of inspiration (if that's the word) at the office to fuel it. Mostly the dragging deal with Danscombe.

Those erotic dreams still fanned my sleep on a regular basis. Many of them, just like that vivid scene from Thailand, harked back to my youth. When I thought about it in the clear light of day, I was very well aware that I was now free to go out and live any fantasy I damn well pleased. But the responsible adult in me pushed back. Afraid to get it wrong. Afraid to embarrass myself. Afraid of rejection. Afraid of some rebound thing that would lead to my getting hurt.

It was easier to get into a close relationship with my laptop and my phone. They were unpredictable, sure, but they never left you bored. No time to think about the stuff you didn't want to think about.

There was nothing healthy about the way I lived that winter. I ate even less than before, and rarely sat down if I did manage to grab a snack. I hardly shopped — George had mostly taken care of that — so the kitchen at home stayed empty. And I never did get that hair makeover.

Nor did I let my friends or family distract me. Of course, there was no way I could keep my divorce secret from my parents, my kids or my sister Jess. But I was always the strong one, brushing off their offers to keep me company, bring me food, keep me busy. Jess dragged me out a couple of times, but I didn't like how it turned into a victim thing. I really wasn't one for 'forget about him, look at that!' and 'treat yourself, you're worth it!' kinds of nights on the town. Nor was some stupid facial treatment going to quick-fix me. I was too good at spotting superficiality for my own good.

Seeing Harriet and Luke didn't necessarily improve my sense of wellbeing. Harriet was a medical freshman at Tennessee State, and Luke still a couple of years away from an engineering degree at Georgetown. It was nice when they came home, but then the nest seemed emptier than ever when they were gone again. Luckily, they were more interested in road-tripping up and down the coast with their college buddies during the winter vacation, so I didn't get those visits unless one of them was passing through town for a night or two. I felt guilty for not missing them more, but grateful that their lives were busy enough for them not to pressure me about anything. They were good kids, and I was happy they didn't lumber themselves with my issues.

I needed a *real* sense of purpose, and work was always ready to offer me that. I was in the office right through Christmas and New Year, agreeing only to a quick family lunch on Christmas Day. Allowing myself to stop for a couple of hours while somebody else cooked, I gobbled up almost three plates of turkey and vegetables. My parents looked on in wonder.

"Have you eaten nothing in the last week?" raged my mother.

"Sure, of course!" I replied through a mouthful of fluffy potato. "This is just *really* good, Mom."

Her eyes narrowed. She was no fool.

"Laura, you've got to start taking care of yourself properly. My daughter does *not* starve just because some guy was a jerk."

I nodded that time, and knew she was more than right, but went straight back to my old ways when I got home. It was nothing to do with thinking I had to get wafer-thin, or anything like that. I was just in a funk.

If I'd had a boring job, I'd probably have snapped out of the low in no time at all. But the thing about being 'empowered' or being in a 'leadership role' is that you *don't* have a boring job. At least not in the sense that you're filing your nails and contemplating the office artwork all day. You might have a PA, but you also have a permanent excuse not to take care of yourself.

All the more so given that the deal with Danscombe was completely in the doldrums, and we were working like crazy to bring it back to life. London had seemingly issued a strict instruction not to compromise on the deadline thing whatsoever. Andre had tried every one of his tricks to get them to take that ten percent, but he'd hit a wall. Now we were losing money fast, and both Andre and I were hearing all about it from the Board.

We'd spend the early part of the year looking for other ways we could get some advantage from the deal if we gave in to their demands on the price. I'd spend days locked in rooms with our tax experts (or tax-avoidance experts, to be more accurate about it), trying to see where we could tweak a word or two to get a break.

Nothing was working. And by the time the cherry blossoms emerged, we were beginning to lose hope.

"Fucking Danscombe," said Andre on an almost hourly basis. "We *cannot* afford the terms they're proposing. When are they going to see that?"

He was starting to take this personally. I was pretty sure he'd never had a deal stall this long. The only good side to this was seeing him wrestle with the notion of failure. It was exactly what his ego needed, if you asked me. Especially now that Alan, our President, had begun to take a close interest in proceedings.

"And yet we know that they're talking to other companies," Alan would reply. "And we're pretty sure they're being offered a better deal. Danscombe want to go with us, because we have the best reputation. But money talks, and it won't be long before they walk in here and tell us they're going with the cut-price option. This has been going on so long, something has to give."

"They could even walk in with a 24-hour ultimatum," Andre would say. "I can feel it in the air. Those British bastards."

The conversation would go round and round like that, and then, when Alan had left the room, Andre would take out his frustration on me.

"So Laura, how's the divorce going?" he might taunt.

Despite my best attempts to hide my split from George from everybody at work, someone had prised it out of me after a couple of glasses (not Chardonnay, this time — that was tainted) too many at the year-end office party I should never have allowed myself to go to. And now everyone knew all about it, of course.

"Signed and sealed, as I've told you. How's life as a slimy womanizer?"

I'd given up any attempts to engage him in a friendly way long ago. The entire office knew we had to spend a ton of time together and that somehow we made it work professionally, but that this was as far as it went. Just about everyone at Kerstein appreciated that someone stuck with a guy like that for as long as I was had to talk back in order to survive.

They all knew what kind of a guy Andre was. The women my age or older all seemed to have sympathy for the fact that I had to work with someone of his ilk. They saw no appeal in his outer sheen — or at least they *said* they didn't, instead choosing to openly admire my resilience. The younger ones, on the other hand, gave me the cold shoulder. All they saw was an unfeasibly handsome guy, and they envied the time I got to spend with the hunk. As if there was anything to be jealous about.

After all, sex wasn't something I was giving myself any time to think about during my waking hours. Nor to lament.

Not that the outrageous (and outrageously gorgeous) Andre would have been on my list if he were the last guy on earth. I had more self-respect than that. And anyway, I was used to droughts.

That's how my existence looked that April. My job was going in circles. And my life was that job. Simple as that.

I was treading water, going nowhere. Everything seemed to be hanging. I was suspended in meaningless non-achievement. My timeline had become one long lowlight.

And it was only in my dreams that the bubbling cauldron of my lust threatened to overflow.

Chapter V

Just when a hint of spring came into the air, Danscombe dropped a bombshell on us. A rugged and beautiful bombshell named Tommy.

He turned up at our offices on a fresh and sunny Monday morning, without a word of warning. Mark was with him, suddenly looking like a timid shadow. Tommy was well over six feet, and at least nine inches taller than his colleague. The difference was even greater when you took his tight wheat-coloured curls into account.

And the moment he opened his mouth to speak to us, my stomach leapt.

"Good morning," he declared. His strong voice had a rough, potent edge to it, like a megaphone with the volume turned down. "My name's Tommy, and I'll be replacing Daniel from now on. You must be Andre and Laura?"

I barely registered this major turn of events as I reeled from the accent. I'd never met a Scotsman in real life before. This one sounded so much better than the movies. His 'good' rhymed with 'rude', and when he rolled the 'r' in 'morning', it sounded like a tiger purring.

He did it with my name, too. And the moment I heard 'Laurrrra' said that way, I felt my soul wake up for the first time in months.

Thank God I could rely on Andre to do the initial talking at that point. Already quivering from hearing Tommy speak for the first time, and already feeling myself blush as I stared into his fascinating, gunmetal-grey eyes, the feeling that came with that first authoritative handshake was almost too much. Was I supposed to *negotiate* with this man? I wasn't even sure I could find my voice.

"Thanks for joining us, nice to meet you," said Andre, switching on the charm as he took it all in his stride. And then: "Hello Mark, welcome back."

The atmosphere in the room fizzed up in a way that I hadn't felt in the entire negotiation thus far. The reason was simple: Danscombe had just sent in an alpha male who could match Andre. Mark had become almost invisible as these two heavyweights shook hands and sized each other up for the first time. Things had gone up a notch.

As the sun streamed in through the window, I sensed something primal going on. Both men knew they were cut from the same cloth. Where would *that* lead?

I guessed it could go one of two ways. Andre's tactics might change now. He might try to take advantage of the many things he had in common with the newcomer — take him out beer-drinking, watch sports with him, treat him to strippers on company expenses or who knew what else. Either that, or he'd skip the buddy-buddy approach completely, bracing himself for a battle in which his chances were probably even.

Let them sort it out.

My priority was to try to regain my breath, my composure and my self-control as Andre motioned us to take our seats at the table.

I reversed clumsily towards my spot, not wanting to turn my back on the brown-skinned beauty who had just walked into our week unannounced. I was painfully aware that I must look like an awkward schoolgirl. I was quite sure that Tommy's effect on me wouldn't escape Andre's attention, and that he'd remind me of this later.

And there would be no point in trying to deny any teasing — my thoughts right now might as well have been playing out on a Broadway stage. I hadn't given men a waking thought for so many months. I was used to working with a hot guy, but he was enough of a bastard that I could ignore his appealing outward appearance. But today, a hot guy *with a Scottish accent*? Who might *not* be a jerk? I was hopelessly unprepared and out of practice for staying composed in such a moment.

It was a relief to sit down at the table. It offered at least a little protection from what I thought must be the most painfully obvious signs of attraction, which I knew would be an inability to keep my legs still. We got down to business immediately. The meeting began politely, with Andre and Tommy each taking their turn to speak at length. It was like the opening statements in a courtroom drama.

Only Tommy's gaze was more piercing than that of any television lawyer I could ever remember seeing. He addressed both of us in equal measure, glancing in my direction a lot more regularly than Daniel or Mark ever had. When he looked towards Andre I could just about hold it together and pay attention to the words coming at us, but when Tommy's piercing eyes shot over to me, there was no way I could keep my mind on any legalities.

I tensed every muscle not to squirm visibly. For as long as I could politely get away with, I stared at the little red dots on Tommy's navy-blue tie. That way, there would be minimal eye contact to deal with.

While my mushy brain registered that nothing much had changed on the negotiations front, I became hyper-aware of people passing down the hallway outside the glass-fronted conference room. Were my female colleagues walking past a little more often than usual? Were they going slower than might be natural, taking a good long look at the phenomenon as they went? Word was getting around already, wasn't it?

I couldn't believe I'd morphed into a jealous, possessive monster in the space of a few minutes. Me, the woman who worked with Andre and paid him no heed! Now, especially when one of the younger girls in high heels slunk along the glass, I wanted to run out and slap them. It was madness. I didn't recognize myself.

All these reactions might have been instinctive, but they sure as hell weren't logical! There wasn't any way a guy this handsome could be remotely interested in me. He was far too rugged for most Hollywood movies, but if you asked me that was a good thing. I'd have taken him over a polished film star any day.

The whole atmosphere of the meeting, when I could keep my mind on it at all, was pretty neutral. Following the introductions, we merely re-covered a lot of ground we'd already covered with Daniel. For now it seemed less about getting anywhere on the stalemate than about the two lead negotiators feeling each other out. This first round of shadow-boxing was over in a little under forty-five minutes.

The only thing that really struck me was how vague Tommy was about his background. He said he'd recently joined Danscombe, and hid his more distant past in jargon about consulting and projects. It was an oddly muted resume for a man charged with sealing one of his company's biggest deals.

As we all stood up to leave, my legs felt like they'd spent the whole of yesterday running on the treadmill. But it was nothing other than the same panicked reaction my body had given me since I was about twelve. I'd first felt it when one of those hot older guys I never dared speak to passed me in the hallway at school. I'd not known it for a long time, but there was no mistaking that flush going all the way down to my belly. My heart thudded hard.

I watched and waited to see how Andre would end things.

"Been to New York before, Tommy?" he asked casually as he shuffled his papers together. Was this friendly Andre or arms-length Andre? As well as I knew him, I wasn't sure yet.

"I haven't, no," conceded Tommy, looking first at me, then Andre, then me again. "Is it always this warm and sunny in April?"

"Better ask Laura, she grew up here," said Andre. It was markedly more civil behaviour than I was used to from him. I wondered if he sensed it would be in our company's interests to foster good relations between Tommy and I. Maybe he'd noticed something in the air?

That was certainly wishful thinking.

"Definitely not always," I said, feeling the heat in my throbbing throat rising as everyone's gaze turned my way. "It could just as easily be a blizzard outside right now. You're lucky today. Everyone will be in a good mood too."

My words had sounded like a bit of a croak to me, with the drum-beat of my pulsing heart thudding behind them in my head, but thank God I was able to string a sentence together. I hadn't been at all sure what was going to come out in the moment.

And I'd meant what I said about the good vibes in NYC. Those first few sunny days at the end of winter brought out the best in people — even cab drivers. Probably also something primal. The promise of regeneration. Mating season.

"I see," said Tommy, taking a deep breath, which I couldn't help following all the way down his expanding chest, watching the buttons on his crisp, white shirt tense against the inhalation. He looked lean like a man in his early thirties, but I still surmised him to be around forty. His job implied it — and so did the aura of life experience he carried with him. I could see it most in the way he used those eyes of his. No younger man could look you up and down with such assurance.

Wait a second. He *did* just cast his glance down my body, didn't he? I wasn't even sure any more. I'd been too busy watching his shirt stretch when he breathed in. Maybe my mind was playing tricks. Seeing what it wanted to see. I wanted him to stay all day — but I also needed him to get the hell out of here so I could breathe again.

"Well, if you need any tips, just let us know," I volunteered. "There are plenty of great places to be outside in the springtime. Even though it might look like it's all concrete!"

"Thank you, I will," said Tommy, raising an eyebrow as if he wanted to ask something else. But he said nothing further. Disappointing.

"What about nightlife?" asked Andre. "You a whiskey man, Tommy? Man, I love the stuff. And don't all the Scots love it too? Invented it, if I'm not mistaken."

Hah! So Andre was going to try the alpha bro approach after all. Interesting.

"Aye, I'll have a wee dram now and then," replied the Scotsman.

Andre looked confused. I didn't understand Tommy either, but anything that came out of his mouth sounded like sweet music to me. All the better if it was some impenetrable slang.

But it stopped Andre dead in his tracks. He couldn't answer with an invitation to show Tommy the city's best bars and dens of iniquity after dark. Because my negotiating partner wasn't quite sure what had been said.

I darted my eyes back and forth between the two men. Tommy knew exactly what was going on, and I thought I could see a pinch of amusement in his eyes as he watched his counterpart thrown off his plan. It clearly wasn't the first time he'd seen the biggest and loudest of bullies stunned into silence by the power of language. His English may have been an accident of birth, but what an elegant way to shut someone up!

Strike one to Tommy.

He held out his hand to Andre, whose eyes flicked over to mine as if searching for help. Highly unusual. I gave him nothing. I only noticed, all of a sudden, that my hands were clasped behind my back and that I was tapping my right shoe on the floor.

"So...see you tomorrow?" asked Andre as the two shook hands.

"Absolutely," replied Tommy.

He was looking at me, not Andre. My breath hitched as he turned his body to me as well. What was I supposed to do?

I instinctively fished out my right arm and held out my hand, but he was already leaning in. *Shit! Is this going to be some European kissing thing?*

It was, and I froze. Then Tommy brushed each of my cheeks with his. The right one first: warm and sensual. Then the left one: soft and delicious. It wasn't a kiss, exactly. But his scent, close-up, was an assault on my senses. Wood and leather and whiskey and smoke shimmered past my mind's eye — was this how a Scottish pub would smell inside?

And that hand I'd stretched out, and which he'd ignored. I could have let it drop. I could have left it hanging in mid-air. I could have placed it softly on my stomach. But somehow that's not what happened. Instead, I found it touching his waist. I froze for a second time. *What are you doing, Laura?*

Tommy seemed not to feel it, thank God. I prayed Andre hadn't noticed it. Our visitor stood up straight and withdrew with effortless grace. He just nodded to each of us one last time and left the room. Mark followed him out, forgetting his formalities with us entirely. It was like he was under the same spell I was.

I tried to compose myself. Not easy when you're bedazzled, not to mention amused to see your dickhead of a colleague flounder.

Suddenly it felt like I was on Tommy's side. And from a professional point of view, that meant I was going to have to tread mighty carefully from this moment onwards.

Chapter VI

"Well, it's absolutely clear what we have to do."

It was later that same Monday morning. Andre had regained his composure and I was rolling my eyes. Things were completely back to normal, in other words. We were huddled in one of the smaller meeting rooms on our floor, and Andre was trying to lay down the law as he paced around the table. Only this time the conversation wasn't about money or technicalities or delivery times.

"No, Andre," I repeated for the third time. I tried to sound patient and firm, but my heart was nowhere near back to its regular pace yet. It was a long time since it had had such a burst of excitement, and my stomach was still in a knot.

"Look, you want this deal to go through as much as I do," he said, stopping in front of me and narrowing his eyes as he leaned in across the table. "You can make this happen in less than a week. You think I didn't see how he looked at you?"

My heart leapt when he said it. *Aha! You didn't imagine it!* I'd already begun to convince myself that the once-over Tommy had given me had been nothing more than my mind seeing what it wanted to see.

I nearly jumped out of my seat and hugged Andre. But the feeling lasted only a split of a moment. I swallowed hard and said the right thing. Just like I always did. Legal professional and all that.

"You're being crazy. Can we have a serious conversation or shall I just go back to my desk?"

Andre sat down on the chair opposite me. He literally *never* did that. When it came to internal meetings, he was a pacing man. Now he looked like he was actually trying to connect with me. This day was getting weirder.

"Look, you can be the hero here. Just flirt a little. Ask him what his plans for the weekend are. Don't touch him, though. And don't let him touch you. Much."

Now I felt my blood boiling. The *fucker!!* First of all, I wasn't going to start flirting with our biggest potential clients. And second of all, if I did want to do that, no way was *Andre* going to tell me what my dating strategy should be. It made me want to do exactly the opposite of 'don't touch him'. A scenario I was pretty sure would play out in my dreams tonight. I squirmed at the thought.

"I can do without that kind of advice, thank you. And I'm not going to be some kind of pawn in this game. We can win this without that sort of tactic.

"Laura, I know how men are," Andre ploughed on, his forehead creasing with angry impatience. "When he's desperate for you, we can catch him at his weakest. He'll sign anything we want him to. Trust me!"

"No way," I said flatly. I sat back in my chair, folded my arms and fixed my gaze on him. I was secretly enjoying this. I felt wanted, in more ways than one. I almost wanted to string this conversation out just to force Andre to tell me I was attractive. I guess my ego had gotten a little spoilt that morning.

"Nobody on the Board is going to judge you," he pushed. "They'll understand. People who get that far in life know what really makes this world go round."

"I thought it revolved around you?" I said, straight-faced. I was enjoying this even more now. It would pass the time until I could get home and relive the morning's excitement, perhaps with a finger or two in my panties to help me along.

"You need to take this seriously," barked Andre, humourless as ever. "And you owe us one. How many times have you stopped this thing getting over the line with your legal technicalities?"

"Fine, next time we'll forget the law and I'll make sure *you* go to jail. Is that what you want?" I was getting steamy now. "Oh, and I wouldn't be the 'hero' either. I'd be the office slut. You have any idea what women are like in this place? I'm probably the office slut already just for having been in a meeting room with that guy. So don't start billing this as some kind of starring role. I'm too old and wise to fall for that."

Andre paused. He drummed his fingers across the table, as if playing an invisible piano on the surface of the wood. I could see his mind working.

"Yeah, maybe you're right. You're too fucking old for that guy. What was I thinking? He can go out and pick up every college girl in New York. One after the other. All night long. Forget it already."

His game was so damn obvious. Blatant reverse psychology. A laughably unsubtle change of tack. But he was good. The college girl thing. He knew that would strike a nerve with me after the divorce. *Don't let this ape get to you, Laura.*

But even though I knew exactly what he was doing, it was working on me. In an instant my doubts welled up. How could I have thought for a second that a guy of Tommy's stature would give a second thought to a washed-up mom like me? My eyes narrowed and I eyed Andre like a bad-tempered bullfrog.

"I don't need any of this," I declared. "You better be careful I don't walk out on you. And by the way, you might want to start watching what you say to a lawyer. I can do defamation just as well as I can do divorce."

We both knew I wasn't going to sue him. Andre knew he'd always be safe in this company, one way or another. He smiled as though I'd said nothing at all, and pulled out his phone instead. He scrolled for a moment, nodded with satisfaction, tapped a couple of times with his thumb and put the cellphone back on the table. He nodded in the direction of my phone, face down on the table. It vibrated just as he did so.

I sighed. The guy looked so smug at moments like this. They were the only time you'd ever see him grin. That moment when he didn't know what to say to Tommy was a distant memory already. For Andre, it probably hadn't happened at all. Denial and forgetfulness were key ingredients in his confidence.

"One of those pretty young things downstairs has found out his hotel address already. Maybe you could accidentally bump into him?"

Pretty young things. There he went again.

"No, no, NO!!!" I shouted, getting up to leave. I grabbed my phone but no way was I going to look at it. Not right now, at least.

Andre stayed right where he was. He looked entirely comfortable in his chair. And he wouldn't care if a few people in the open-plan office had heard a voice being raised. Our animosity was no secret in this place.

"That's a shame, Laura. I really think you'd enjoy it—"

I was already out of the door, but I heard him. Of course I did. Clearly Andre hadn't missed *my* reaction to Tommy this morning. Yet another button pressed — hot on the heels of the one that had made me wonder if my 'moment' with Tommy was a figment of my imagination.

I was struggling to hold myself together as I headed to the elevator. Shaking, I pushed the button for the ground floor. Fresh air and coffee, that's what I needed.

I hated that Andre was right. I hated that I'd finally met a guy who made me swoon, and that he happened to be a professional relationship of the most delicate order. I hated those 'college girls' Andre invented — and the fact that they'd be the ones Tommy really wanted. The magic of the morning had been ruined and I wasn't looking forward to any of this now.

For the first time, I wasn't sure I could keep going with the negotiation. I thought I could handle being attracted to a client, even if this was something more primal than I'd ever experienced before. But to have Andre watching my interactions like a hawk? All of a sudden I felt like calling in sick. Forever.

I emerged into the foyer and headed straight for the Starbucks branch we had in our lobby. Like an alcoholic keeps the neighbourhood bottle store going, my workaholism probably made sure this place was always in profit. They all knew me by sight, though I'd never really done any small talk with them.

Today the Asian-looking girl named Thanh (according to her name badge) was on duty. I thought she might be from Thailand, something like that. She smiled as always as she went to fix my latest installment of latte. I tried to smile back, but the morning's roller-coaster had really drained me. I couldn't hide it. I just stared dumbly at the rows of coffee mugs behind her, lost.

"Are you okay?" she asked as she rang up my bill.

I must have looked really bad. I could feel a tear trying to well up in my eye, but I fought it off with a sniff.

"Oh, I think I'm just catching a cold," I coughed unconvincingly.

"In this weather? But it's just warming up!"

"Well, I'm not always so lucky with stuff," I murmured as I scratched in my purse for some money.

It was too loaded a remark for someone wanting to lie low. She cocked her head sympathetically as I handed her a couple of bills.

"Maybe you should get some rest," she smiled. "Then you'll get well quick. I'm sure your work can wait."

I blinked at her as I took my paper cup. I couldn't think of anything to say. Just a minute ago I'd thought about signing myself off sick. Now a complete stranger was saying the same thing.

Well, a complete stranger who knew very well how unsociable the times of my comings and goings from this building were. She'd been working here at least since the divorce, if not longer. She'd watched me through that darkest winter.

Maybe it was a sign. A sign that I should take that cup of coffee and leave the office for today.

The thought made me feel as rebellious as if I'd asked Tommy to bend me over the conference table and take me from behind. I couldn't honestly remember ever having been sick from work. I could barely even remember my last vacation.

But there was nothing on earth that made me want to go back up to my desk, where my laptop sat, password-locked and waiting impatiently for my return. Along with a particularly aggressive Andre, and probably about forty-five nosy female colleagues wanting to suck up every detail I cared to share about Tommy. I didn't have the stomach for that right now, much less for meeting the Scotsman again the next day.

Yes, I was feeling pretty green, all told.

"I think...maybe you're right…" I said to Thanh.

She just smiled again.

I gave her a weak smile of thanks, took one more uncertain glance at the elevator, shrugged and picked up my handbag. Then I walked towards the glass doors leading out into the busy street. *Fuck 'em.* I'd tell Alan later. And *he* could tell Andre. Mr 'Don't touch him'. No, I didn't want to see his boarish face any time soon. He'd gone too far today.

Things had sunk to a new low with Andre, that was for sure. I'd developed a thick skin for my dealings with him, sure, and wasn't surprised by his completely inappropriate suggestions. But today he'd even managed to steal my fantasies. How was I supposed to think about Tommy in the same way after the conversation we'd just had? He'd suddenly been labelled as a work responsibility. Just another task, numbered and categorized, in our project management platform.

Even though I wasn't going to have anything to do with my negotiating partner's dumbass plan, how could I relive this morning's intoxicating first meeting without thinking about signatures on contracts? The wonder had been killed already. That was the part that really got to me. I could feel myself frowning as I walked towards the subway station.

The traffic and the noise and people all faded to grey as I walked along on autopilot. I was astounded at myself. I might, once upon a time, have missed a day for sickness, but I'd never spontaneously walked out like that. I thought I'd held it together pretty well upstairs, but clearly I was in a pretty bad way if I was walking around New York in such a daze.

I had a fleeting thought to look at my phone, see where Tommy was staying, go over there and let him touch me every way a woman can possibly imagine. I might get fired, but it would be a hell of a fun way to answer Andre's proposals.

The fleeting thought passed — I guess I wasn't feeling quite crazy enough to give it serious consideration. But then came another spontaneous move — or at least some part of my subconscious did. I took the bus home.

Travelling on the bus would take almost thirty minutes longer, but I didn't feel like I wanted to go into the dark, smelly tube that was the subway. Not on such a fine day as this. The sun was still shining bright and staying above ground might help me clear my head.

The ageing bus jerked its way along, stopping for lights and people all the time. I looked out of the left-side window, gazing at the honking taxis and storefronts and street signs without really taking anything in. The world was still doing its thing. My crisis in the office meant nothing to anybody out here. All the heart and soul I gave to that job was positively meaningless to the restless city beyond this bus window.

Work had become my world. Yet the world couldn't have cared less about my work.

Why didn't I enjoy myself more? Create some worthwhile memories? *Live* more? Then at least *somebody* would be having fun. Suffering only made sense if someone might benefit from it, and suddenly I was questioning whether all those emails and meetings did anything real for anybody.

But maybe that was just my bad mood talking. I was emotional, after all, and I knew it. I'd met the most beautiful (but of course untouchable) man I'd ever seen, then been attacked by the worst of bullies, all in the same morning. It added up to a glum, guilty Laura.

I couldn't work out where the guilt came from. Maybe it was some divorce leftover. Or maybe it just felt like it belonged somewhere in all this emotional spewing. Whatever, I didn't see how I was going to shake it any time soon.

The bus reached my stop. But the ride hadn't yet done anything for my spirits. I thought about staying aboard to the very end of the line, just for the sake of it. But a voice was telling me not to let the funk take me down. I dragged myself off the vehicle, but my legs were lead when I reached the sidewalk. I watched the bus rumble off into the distance.

Did I still have my handbag? Suddenly I didn't trust myself. But yes, there it was, thank God. Under my arm as always. Just another piece of routine that I wore as thoughtlessly as a pair of socks.

It was around eleven-thirty in the morning. I wasn't sure I'd ever been here on a working weekday before, what with my inability to claim the vacation I was entitled to. The street was unexpectedly peaceful.

This was obviously a quiet time of day in my neighbourhood. Kids were in school, I supposed, while other folks were at work and it wasn't quite lunchtime yet. Only pensioners and the self-employed (plus the odd freakout case like me) were wandering around on the sidewalks. Hmm. I wondered if I should go and get drunk. Wasn't that what people did in these situations? And hey, I wasn't *really* sick. Not in the physical sense.

If I went home now, what would I do with myself? Rage about Andre? Or try my best to have an Andre-free dream, preferably with that Scotsman in a starring role? I'd probably just get caught somewhere in between the two extremes and have an unpleasant experience.

Maybe a little drink wouldn't hurt. Might get me in a more positive mood. But where to go during the daytime around here? I wasn't used to that kind of challenge.

A short walk up the hill, past my house and towards a cluster of businesses, revealed that my part of town was actually pretty nice at this time on a weekday. It had enough hipsters and non-working parents, it seemed, to keep a low-key hum going even at this quiet, in-between hour. And it wasn't hard to find an establishment that slotted in somewhere between coffee shop and wine bar.

"I'll have a Prosecco, please," I said to the waiter after I claimed a seat at a small table next to the floor-to-ceiling window.

"Well then, that's on us!" he said. Everything about him was casual and friendly, as befitted the place. He wore a black t-shirt and black jeans, and could easily have been mistaken for a customer if the t-shirt didn't have the name of the place neatly stencilled on the left breast. He had curious eyes, scruffy blonde hair, sharp features and a beard that was just beginning to take shape.

"What? I don't, I mean—"

I thought I sounded impossibly dopey. But he smiled.

"First alcoholic drink order of the day is always on the house," he grinned. "But shhh, don't tell anybody. Otherwise all the moms will be fighting their way in here for bubbly before they pick up kids from school. It could be mayhem."

In spite of myself, I smiled. "Well then, thanks! Although, I'm a mom too, I have to admit."

He raised his left eyebrow with interest. His right one went down at the same time, making him look even more amused and confused.

"Really? So where are the little rascals then?"

"Little? Oh no...haha...they're in college!"

"Yeah, right. Sure they are. And I suppose you're 95!"

My ego was enjoying this. Not for the first time today, I could feel it sitting up and taking notice.

"Well, it's the truth! My daughter Harriet is at Tennessee State and my son Luke is studying in Georgetown."

The waiter, who must have been around thirty and was looking more attractive by the second, coughed. "But you don't look...hmm, I'm gonna need a minute to take that in. Be right back with that drink."

I smiled my very first smile of the day as I watched him turn and walk away. I didn't care if he said things like that to all the women who came in here — hitting up this wine bar was the best decision I'd made since getting out of bed.

"Any particular reason for the morning alcohol?" he asked when he brought the fizz-filled flute over on a tray and placed it neatly in front of me. Even the sight of it had a calming effect on me.

"Hey, it's only ten minutes till noon!" I sparred back playfully. "But no. Nothing special. Well, apart from the fact that I'm off work sick."

I gave him a wink as I said the last part. Something about this conversation was clearly making me feel playful.

He touched his nose conspiratorially.

"Well you have the right medicine, I'd say," he whispered in a fun voice. "Holler if you need anything, okay?"

I nodded and let him go back to his other customers. He'd given me plenty of what I needed already. A little humanity never hurts, does it? I took a sip of my drink safe in the knowledge that I would have a spring in my step when I stood up again.

I took about an hour over my drink, enjoying the special unwind that comes with unexpected bonus time and a dash of alcohol. I started off wondering how the office was dealing with my failure to return to my desk. Had anyone noticed yet, or would they all just assume I was in meetings? I wasn't worried about being in trouble — I was too senior for that — but whenever my absence was noted it would certainly come as a shock.

Whatever, no rush.

The deeper I sipped into my drink, the less I thought about work. And the more I thought about Tommy.

Well, Tommy *was* work, of course. That was a rather serious problem for my professional focus, even if there was no chance of Tommy returning my interest. But in my imagination, he was nothing to do with my day job. There, he was freely available and very interested. So was I, of course — I didn't need any imagination for that to be true.

Come to think of it, I might very well expect to 'accidentally bump into him' in a place just like this. Although not in this exact part of town — it was a little too suburban. In any case he'd be off sightseeing today, wouldn't he?

Wherever he was, I doubted he'd be stressing about our next meeting. Something about him had already told me that he was going to get his way in the end. And that he knew this as fact. That's probably just the thing that had made Andre turn into an even more obnoxious beast than usual.

Once I got into my second glass of bubbling balm, I actually started to *see* Tommy. Wasn't that him that just stepped off a bus on the other side of the road? The guy had a similar build, didn't he? Then, when the sun moved lower and I could see shadows passing the window before I saw their owners, I kept holding my breath when I saw that of a tall-looking man. And for a moment I would dare to believe it could be him.

Don't be an idiot Laura. Stop hallucinating like a silly teenager!

At least I was sufficiently aware to know that it was my mind playing tricks. Just like it had done first thing that morning, when I'd thought Tommy might have been showing a primal attraction to me — hah! I might have been in a better mood now that I was sinking some alcohol, but at the same time my rational brain was kicking back in big-time. After all, it had taken a good part of the morning off.

Still, I couldn't prevent myself from sneaking a peek at the information Andre had sent over earlier. He hadn't been kidding — our sleuths really did seem to have found the guy's current address in no time at all. Tommy was staying at a well-known, upmarket hotel in a classy neighbourhood not far from the office. With his long legs, I imagined he could stroll to our meetings from there in fifteen minutes.

Even Tommy's room number was there. 932. I put the phone away before I decided to try anything really stupid.

I stayed in my seat the whole afternoon, slipping in and out of harmless reverie. That, and enjoying the occasional spirit-lifting visit from the effusive young waiter while I sipped. I ordered a salad and munched it slowly, revelling in the strange but pleasant sensation of not eating at a desk. And the unusual feeling of not trying to type emails with one hand while handling egg noodles with the other. Considering how upset I'd been when I left the office, I was surprised how good I felt just a short while later.

Once the sun went down, I decided it must be time to move on. As you'd expect for a bright day like that so early in the year, it suddenly felt extra-cold when darkness settled in the late afternoon. It felt like it was time for a shift in scenery.

Sure, I could have stayed and daydreamed some more, or even flirted with the waiter until closing time — only a few more hours! — but by now I had a knot in my stomach that urgently needed to be dealt with. The kind of knot you could only handle in the privacy of your own home. And I was definitely in a good enough mood to deal with it now.

I staggered home, and it wasn't because of the stiffening breeze. The bubbly had done the trick, and I was ready to enjoy a little me-time. It was far too long since I'd done that. But then, it was far too long since I'd had the kind of inspiration I'd had today. Or a tight kernel of need in my midriff.

Merrily I slipped that little metal key into the slot and let myself in. It was the first time since *that* night with George that I'd done so with anything like the same anticipation. Only this time I knew it would end well. Because I didn't need to count on anybody else.

I went to the kitchen, grabbed a glass of water and kicked off my shoes at the bottom of the stairs. I was heading for the bedroom. Just me, my imagination and my pink vibrator. 'Accidentally bump into him.' Hmm, that was something to work with. I would just have to try not to think about who that idea had come from.

The bed looked more inviting than it had done for a long time. I smoothed out my skirt and sat down on the edge of it. I gently slid open the bottom drawer. There he was. Long, bright and very, very patient. Mmm. I took the toy with my fingers and rolled it onto the palm of my hand with a wicked smile.

What was that?

I could swear I heard something. Just a tiny dull thud — *thump* — the neighbour's cat on another one of his raids, probably. Or something blowing around in the wild wind outside? But the sound had seemed closer than outside. Less distant than I wanted to think about.

I brushed it off. Nothing was going to interfere with my fun plans right now. But just to be on the safe side, I got up and walked onto the landing outside the bedroom door. From there, I could see all the way down the stairs to the front door. Clearly I hadn't failed to close it. Good.

I shrugged and went back into my lair. I drew the curtains but kept the door open. It was another thing I'd come to enjoy about living on my own. No need to hide anything from anyone.

I decided to stick with the work clothes. Everything felt naughtier that way, especially considering where I'd met Tommy. All I did was loosen my bra before I lay down in the middle of my bed and reached inside my blouse for my left nipple. For as long as I could remember, I'd always liked starting there. And today there was definitely no hurry. I thought about a scene where I went and knocked on that hotel room door — 932 — but couldn't quite shake the reality that he would laugh in my face.

Instead, I settled on the idea that I was going to 'bump into' Tommy at the same little Prosecco-purveying establishment I'd just been in. Maybe my waiter friend would have a supporting role to play as well. We'd see how things unfurled.

Rapidly the teasing on my tits spread fire to the area between my legs. I'd barely begun to formulate a scene for myself when I switched to tweaking and twisting my right nipple with my left hand, leaving my right hand free to travel inside my skirt.

But just as I began to moan out loud, my senses losing themselves in a horny, hypnotic haze, something didn't feel right. Was that another noise? A footstep?

It's just the cat again. Continue.

No, wait. That was too loud to be the cat.

Who just breathed?

My blood ran cold and my fingers held still.

At just the moment I dared to open my eyes, the lights went out in the bedroom.

And before I could wriggle or cry, I felt the sharp sting of a slap across the face.

Chapter VII

The blow didn't knock me out. Not physically, at least. But it did send me a hard message, wrapped up in searing pain: this was *not* a dream. My pleasure had been shattered. Something abominable was happening to me, and it was real.

My primal response, rightly or wrongly, was not to resist. Instinct told me I was up against a strength far greater than mine, and that struggling would only make things worse. The pain howled right through my skull, reverberating like a coyote's cry in the night. My eyes seemed to spin in their sockets and both my ears rang with a powerful screech.

What the fuck was going on? I was under attack in my own home. As I processed this shocking new reality my fingers curled tight around my pelvic bone, my back arched in tensed fear and I stopped breathing. Moments after the strike to my face, a powerful weight locked my thighs together, squeezing dull pain into the clawed hand that had frozen in my twisted panties. Moving was out of the question.

Just as I registered that it was a kneeling person locking my legs where they were, something or someone tugged my left hand out of my bra and hurled it down onto the mattress so hard that it bounced. That hand was free to fight, to hit, to scratch — but whoever had so roughly tossed it aside seemed sure that it wouldn't do so. And they were right.

Hands clamped tightly around my neck. I could barely swallow or breathe. The thumbs pressed deep into the soft, vulnerable flesh on either side of my throat, while the fingers dug into the back of my neck with such force that I dared not even attempt to move my head. *Fuck!*

It was the first time in my life that I'd ever been attacked. I'd never experienced so much as an ambush in the school playground. Now that thing that happened to people in the newspapers was happening to me. In my very own home. Who was doing this? And *why*? Why at that moment? The only late weekday afternoon in just about forever that I would be at home?

Next, cold metal in my mouth. Something spherical. Roughly forced in through my lips, and then beyond my teeth, which an insistent thumb prised apart. The weight on my legs and the hands on my neck hadn't moved at all: Jesus, there had to be *two* of them!

There was no doubt about it — I could feel a second distinct weight shifting on the mattress near my left shoulder. If I felt thoroughly overpowered before, I felt sickeningly weak now. How many more assailants were in my pitch-black room? Had my entire house been taken over? My heart lurched anew.

It was too late now to decide to cry out. Between the giant marble that gagged me and the hands on my neck, it was all I could do just to get air into my lungs. Half-choking, I couldn't articulate anything more than grunts. I had no experience of being gagged, but what they'd done to my mouth made me feel more powerless than the collection of strong forces that held me down.

The hands around my neck suddenly yanked me upwards, jerking me into a sitting position.

"Get her naked," urged a heavy, masculine whisper. It had an unmistakably New York accent.

This was it. I was about to be raped. Gang-raped.

No! I couldn't be that woman. Anger rose within me and I tried to twist myself free. But it was pathetic. I could barely budge a millimetre against the vice-like grip that held my legs and my throat down. No chance. And that was before the second intruder moved around behind me, yanked my right wrist out of my underwear, gathered up the left one and clamped them together behind my back. He held them there, twisting the skin so tight it burned, with what felt like a giant's pair of hands.

The man in front of me — the one who'd just hissed the command to strip me — let go of my throat and dropped his fingers onto the collar of my blouse. Then, without a moment's pause, he simply ripped it open. I could hear some of the buttons land on the carpet as they flew in all directions across the room.

I wished I could scream, and loud enough that half of New York would come running to my rescue. But all I could let out now were frenzied, tremulous snorts through my nose. I snatched the breaths back up almost as soon as they were out, like a steam train dragging itself up to speed.

The attacker in front of me then proceeded to tear my bra in two. He grabbed the side of each cup and simply pulled it apart. The remains of the garment fell in my lap. I screamed at the humiliation, but the protest came out as nothing more than a gurgle from deep inside my throat. I could feel more and more saliva coursing around the ball gag. That thing seemed to swell bigger and bigger by the moment.

"We can leave the shirt like that," he said. "The tits are clearly visible."

What? Why were they interested in how I *looked*? How twisted a rape was this going to be? Were the sickos planning on taking pictures? My panic doubled at this new unknown.

"Yeah, good," said the one behind me, also in an aggressive whisper. This guy's accent was harder to place, but it certainly didn't sound like he'd grown up round here. Whatever. I just wanted both of them to crawl the fuck back to whatever den they came from.

They were no more than a duo. As my eyes grew just a little more assured in the dark and the pain from that first strike subsided, I began to feel sure I was only dealing with a pair of attackers. In my bedroom, at least.

While the tight lock on my wrists from behind stayed steady, the brute sitting on my thighs wriggled his weight down towards my ankles, pulling down both my skirt and panties as he went. My upper body was in too tight a lock and my kayak-paddler position simply too awkward to kick out as the load on my upper legs lightened. As I felt my painfully shy body ruthlessly exposed, I stopped wanting to look at his dark outline. I closed my eyes tight, hoping this would be over quickly.

When he'd shifted almost all the way down to my feet, the New Yorker lifted his weight for a fraction of a second — far too little for me to react — and grabbed me by the ankles.

"Down," he said to the other guy.

His accomplice seemed to understand perfectly. He separated my wrists so that he was holding one in each of his bear-like hands, and forced them around the side of my body. And he didn't let up until they were across the other side of me. Then he brought them together again, just beneath my freshly bared breasts, and once more clamped both his hands around mine. There was no sense in straining — I could feel the guy had plenty more power in reserve. The foreign guy pressed up behind me was a living, breathing pair of handcuffs.

Then he gave himself some space and hoiked my torso towards him with a swift jerk. I could do nothing but succumb to the sudden force, and my back thudded down onto the bed. It was sticky and wet there, a puddle of fear I'd already sweated out on the covers in the first moments of the attack. Wheezing and coughing behind my gag, I prayed again for this ordeal to be over soon.

He held me down by the wrists once more, pressing them hard into my kidneys. As if working in stereo, his partner went to work immediately on the next maneuver. He lifted my legs in the air, perpendicular to the bed, and roughly pushed what was left of my skirt and panties off first one foot, then the other. He tossed them away towards the bathroom door. I no longer tried to wriggle. That surge of rebellion had left me.

Apart from my open blouse and my stockings, I was now stripped bare. Ridiculously, I could feel myself blushing.

I braced myself. This was surely the moment that the first of them would enter me against my will. When I would become—

"Stand up!" said the guy who sounded like he'd never left Brooklyn, letting go of my legs. "And don't try anything."

I was allowed to sit up again, but with the second guy still holding my hands tight to my midriff, I didn't see how I *could* try anything. But my mind was flying now. What was the hold-up with the rape? Did they want to take me somewhere else? Was it...not happening?

Should I hope or should I dread?

I wriggled my waist slowly towards the edge of the bed, my upper body still held firm from behind. Then, clumsily,

I managed to swing my legs over the side and reach the floor with my feet.

Just as I'd been instructed to do, I stood up.

The attacker with the gorilla hands stood up with me, pulling my wrists down to my sides and holding them there. There was still no way I was escaping a grip like that.

The local guy had also gotten to his feet. He stood close enough that I could hear his rasping breath and smell that he was a smoker. I could tell that he wasn't especially tall — in fact he barely had an edge on me — but that he had a definite bulk of muscle. More than that, I could not see in the dark.

He seemed to look me up and down. Terrified and unsure of what his next move might be, I dared not breathe. He reached out and re-arranged the two halves of my blouse so that they weren't covering any part of my breasts. What was happening? Why this careful dress-up doll game? A new and terrifying thought struck me: they weren't going to rape me, but take photos of me and put them on the internet. I cringed and prayed again.

I was too afraid to think about crying.

"Got the coat?" asked the man behind me. He sounded a little more relaxed now that I was subdued and on my feet.

"Yeah, she's ready for it. We need to get going."

Were we really going somewhere? Was I going to be spared? I dared not think that way. Maybe they were just delaying the inevitable. My mind was in danger of meltdown.

The local guy in front of me reached over to the end of the bed and grabbed a garment.

"Put your arms into the coat," he said, holding it open in front of me. It had to be the thin, knee-length one I'd gotten into the habit of wearing at this time of the year. They must have gotten it from the closet in the entrance hallway, the fucking intruders. "Spin her round."

Releasing only one hand at a time, they slowly rotated me and got me into the coat. The synthetic material felt cool and strange on my largely bare skin. This coat didn't have buttons, only a belt. The short New Yorker pulled it closed, taking care for the buttonless blouse underneath to stay exactly as he'd arranged it — breasts clearly visible — and did up the belt around the waist.

I was desperately confused, but before I could come up with any theories about what was happening, the guy behind me started pushing me roughly towards the bedroom door. I knew where everything was — this was my own house, supposedly — but for strangers they seemed to have very good vision in the dark, presumably unfamiliar house. Neither of them so much as stumbled.

I was made to walk down the stairs towards the front door, the New Yorker leading the way and the other guy providing his steadfast rearguard handcuffs service.

"Shoes on," said the leader, who seemed to know exactly where I'd kicked them off when I'd come home. Just how long had they been watching me? It chilled me to think they might already have been inside the house when I'd stumbled in from the wine bar, merry and horny.

I did as I was told. It was still more than dark enough in the hallway for me not to see anything properly, although a little light from the streetlamps crept in through the small window above the door and let me see the local guy's stocky silhouette a little better.

"Time to take the gag out," whispered the voice behind me.

Was this going to be my chance to scream for help?

"Yeah, just as soon as I remind her of a few things," murmured the New Yorker, allowing just a little of his deep voice to be heard above whisper-level. "You're about to go for a walk with us. Under that coat, you are basically naked. I don't need to remind you of that, do I?"

I shook my head. My jaw was aching for a release from the position it had been forced into.

"So," he continued. "One of us will be walking with an arm around your waist at all times. It'll be just like we're a couple in love, understand? But your escort will always have a hand on the belt of that coat, see? And if you make one false move, or scream, or say anything you shouldn't, that coat is going to fly open. Your body will be exposed to all of New York. People will take pictures and tweet that slutty torn-blouse look. So I suggest you behave real nice when we're outside in public."

Real nice. He drawled the words slowly and sweetly, like someone might read tempting treats off a dessert menu.

I closed my eyes in frustration, acutely aware of what brilliance lay behind his instructions. It didn't take much thought to see that it was a watertight master plan. One that forced me to obey without any need for violence.

Sure, of course they'd get arrested if they exposed me in public and I explained the situation to the police. But for that to happen, I'd have to be willing to be nude on the streets of my own city. During rush hour. And there was the distinct possibility that they could run away with the coat before anybody caught them. What woman would take that risk?

Not me. I would obey. As long as I was bare beneath that coat, I'd walk by their sides like a good little girl. They didn't even need me to confirm that fact. *Fuckers!*

I gurgled a consenting sort of noise, which seemed to satisfy them. The same hand that had shoved the ball into my mouth now reached around from behind and forced a thumb and a finger between my teeth. I could barely open my mouth any wider than it was already, but somehow he wiggled it out.

The relief on my jaw was so intense it brought tears to my eyes. I was actually happy for a second. Bad situation, great moment.

"One last thing," said the hometown boy. "We're putting a pair of glasses on you. They're going to blur your vision so you can't see us. From the outside, they look like perfectly normal lenses. You'll see major objects when you're walking along, but I'd say it's another good reason to hold onto your escort.

"You so much as touch those glasses and your coat flies open, understand?" added the other guy.

Helpless frustration welled inside of me, but I nodded and murmured a timid yes. These two had thought of everything. Nobody passing us in the street was going to have the first clue I was a prisoner. Nor could I tell them. Nor would I ever find out what my kidnappers looked like. It was genius.

"All right, Laura. Then let's go."

My blood ran cold. *Laura*. They knew my name. This wasn't random.

I didn't have any time to think further before he opened my front door to the gusty street outside.

Chapter VIII

For the next couple of minutes, all my energy went into the basics of moving forwards without ending up in a disrobed heap on the ground. Guided by the second guy's arm, which felt every bit as strong as his hands had been, I took an uncertain step towards the door. Over my threshold, and out into the city.

Straight away I could tell that the glasses were just like they had said. There was no way I could see details, but shapes and outlines were easy to make out. I could also tell what was near and what was far — the distance from my door to the sidewalk looked entirely familiar. I could also see the second guy's figure for the first time, now that he was at my side and we had streetlamps. But I couldn't discern much except that he was a lot taller than his partner in crime.

It was strange to have my hands free and my aching mouth suddenly bereft of that monstrous object inside it. There was almost nothing between me and freedom. Nothing except the arm around my waist. He had the end of the belt clasped firmly in his palm and his thumb hooked into the loop that held the coat closed. And the belt wasn't especially tight, either. One tug in any direction and I'd be exposed. *Don't trip up, Laura. Walk steady. Concentrate.*

Panic overcame me as I heard my front door get pulled closed behind me. Where were my keys? Was I locked out, or had they taken them? The not-knowing pushed me to close to hyperventilation. Even if I escaped from their clutches right now, how would I get back into my house? I had no sanctuary to which I could flee. It already felt like the nightmare that wouldn't — couldn't! — ever end. Glum resignation was all I could think of.

I didn't know what my fate was. But I felt like it was now sealed. Sealed with the click of that front door latch.

We turned right out of the gate, walking three abreast down the slight incline away from my house. Just a couple and their friend, probably on their way to a start-of-week drink, right? What could look more natural?

Going down the street in the glasses quickly became easy. It wasn't the kind of blurring that made you feel sick or stumble or lose your balance. Nothing was going to happen that would make anyone think 'hey, that woman might be in trouble.'

I almost wished I *would* trip up. Because without an accident, my self-consciousness would keep me imprisoned. Just as they'd planned.

The outline of a person walked past us, a dog-shape straining at its leash in front of her. Its female voice greeted the innocent-looking party heading in the opposite direction, probably with a smile. Couldn't she figure out something wasn't right? Couldn't she smell the fear?

It seemed like nobody in this whole vast city could sense my desperation. We must have gone past dozens of security people outside stores. Maybe even a police officer had walked by at some point. If I could have seen who was who, I could have opened my mouth. My escorts would never have carried out their threats if I called out to an NYPD representative! But I just couldn't make out enough details.

Apart from robbing me of decent sight, the glasses went a long way towards ruling out a passer-by making a spontaneous intervention. Because nobody was going to be able to see the fear in my eyes and sense something was wrong.

I wondered how many times I myself might have scurried past some deadpan soul who was actually living through an abduction. If it were executed as cleverly as this one was, how would anybody ever guess? Who could possibly have guessed that I was essentially naked beneath this perfectly understandable springtime coat? How would they hear that sharp intake of breath that came every time a gust of wind threatened to lift its thin hem?

I was terrified of being naked in public. Even a flash brought on by a blast of breeze would be a catastrophe for me. That girl in the short blue dress, the lustful one who'd been so careless in the hostel? She was long gone. Now she only came out to play in dreams.

We walked on, block after block, zigzagging more than seemed necessary. Not once did we alter our formation, except when the New York guy stepped out of the way to make room for another unsuspecting passer-by. I clung tight to my escort, nervous that even a genuine misunderstanding would result in my belt getting pulled loose. I was in constant fear of somebody trying to push between us. It was around six o'clock in the evening and people were walking in all directions.

Yet not one of them had the slightest doubts about our trio. It was the perfect crime. Broad daylight, in every sense but the literal. My captors were letting my own fears do all the work for them. And having us walk in public was actually better for that purpose than bundling me into a car. A vehicle in the dark would have offered me a lot more privacy. I might have been more troublesome to them in such a space than here on the sidewalk.

They weren't saying a word. But since nobody on the street was going to watch us for more than a few seconds, the fact that our group wasn't saying anything to each other wouldn't have struck anybody as unusual. I assumed I was meant to keep with the silence. Until I could work out some better plan, I would have to go along with things. I kept my mouth shut and walked.

I think I began to grind my teeth. Partly to give my jaw a workout after the spell with the gag, but mostly because of the anxiety.

After a while it became hard to figure out exactly where we might be. I thought I knew my neighbourhood, but with all the turning and the fact that street-signs (and anything else I might want to read) were blurred out of my vision, I was already feeling lost. And by now we'd probably gone far enough away from my house that it would be a part of town I usually traversed underground.

But after a few more minutes I began to get the impression we were heading towards the heart of the city. Towards the area where I worked. After another few blocks I became sure of it. Familiar sequences of colour on storefront signs. The outline of a subway entrance just where I expected one. Big streets just where big streets ought to be. This was familiar ground.

So then, there was every chance of bumping into a colleague right now. Didn't these hoodlums have any fear of *that* happening? Maybe they didn't know where I worked. Maybe they didn't even know who I was. No, wait — one of them had called me Laura. I'd almost forgotten that scary fact. Maybe I'd tried to shut it out of my mind.

Now that I had little else to do but think, the questions tumbled through my brain. Was I really something more than just a random victim? Did this whole ugly adventure go beyond my merely getting unlucky? Or had they done their homework well? Why would anyone want to kidnap *me*? There were people far richer and with infinitely more interesting secrets. And most women were a lot more beautiful than I was.

And yet, I hadn't really been hurt or violated. Was this, in some way I couldn't yet fathom, strictly business for somebody? I didn't know what to hope for.

What would happen if someone I knew came over to me on the street? I'd lived in New York City all my life. Even outside of colleagues, I bumped into people all the time. Usually folks I'd ignored for too long, while I'd been sinking deeper into my work-swamp. But surely the game would be up if some spritely soul came bounding over for a catch-up? Or someone from my floor wondering where I'd been all afternoon? What was *I* supposed to do if they did? Act natural? Tell the person these two thugs were my new beau and his buddy?

But I was a shitty actor. Nobody would buy a line like that.

Or would the guys do the talking, and tell them I'd gone mute? Nobody was going to believe that either. Surely they would smell a rat! But I wished I'd had a briefing.

I felt like anything I did or said, I ran the risk of being exposed.

They wouldn't really open your coat, Laura! In the middle of NYC? They're bluffing you!

The voice of reason kept on yelling at me. I was a smart woman. My brain still worked. If I looked at things from their point of view, surely I could see that them exposing me, horrific a prospect as that was for me, would surely be the end of their little jaunt. Once I was naked, with nothing to lose, I would scream and yell to the dozens of people who would be around. They had to know this was the only route things could take if they loosened my belt.

And yet that irrational kernel of fear held me back like their hands around my throat had held me down. These men were daring and confident. Maybe they *would* do it.

It wasn't as though I could forget just how close I was to being naked. With every step the coat's inner lining chafed gently at my nipples. Each footfall was another gentle pull of the material on the bare skin of my butt. Constant reminders. The danger was too real and too present for me to think straight.

One thing did hit me, though. If my feeling about exactly where we were was correct, then we were somewhere very close to Tommy's hotel. If only I could 'bump into him' now! He would muscle those two out of the way and just scoop me up, coat and all. With one arm under my thighs and one behind my shoulders, he'd cradle me away to safety with my modesty intact.

Another stupid vision. But what a moment it would be for something like that to come true.

Just when it felt like it was almost inevitable that I would run into someone, my captors led me around into what seemed like a narrower, quieter, darker street. We walked along it for maybe a couple of hundred yards, during which time only one car passed us. Away from the crowds, this felt like a place where they could get away with anything. My heartbeat quickened as I sensed we were nearing the end of our journey — one way or another.

Then the guy next to me spoke for the first time in the thirty minutes or so we'd been walking. "Stop. And watch out now. You have steps in front of you. They go down from the sidewalk."

Useful information, if not delivered with any sympathy. I felt for the first step with my foot, glad for a moment that I was being held. My 'date' talked me through each step, until I was so far down that the street seemed level with my eyes.

"Stop. No more steps now."

The place we had reached was particularly dark. Just like it had been with the lights off in my bedroom. I assumed we were in some kind of entrance area. The kind of hollow where bad things happened to women walking on their own.

But there was no sign of any violence. The short guy seemed to be punching a code into a keypad. Three short beeps, then a pause, then two more. A lock clicked and I could make out guy number one opening up a door. Guy number two detached himself and pushed me through it. I heard the two men shuffling in behind me.

We were in an even inkier darkness now. I heard the door close heavily. It sounded like the slam of a vault, echoing through what sounded like a bare, uncarpeted hallway. And then, nothing but their breathing. I felt more scared than at any point since the intruders had first made their presence known on my bed.

"That was very well-behaved, Laura," said the New Yorker. "Grab her hands again!"

Before I could react, the second guy had found my wrists in the dark and squeezed them even tighter than he had at my place. Unnecessarily so. They felt numb almost straight away. And it made something snap inside me. *Fuck him!* I began to wriggle and worm and kick. There was nothing to lose now. We were no longer in public. And anyway, it was totally dark.

Maybe I could use my knee to get one of them in the crotch. I sensed I had a fighting chance here. I was battling blind, but so were they.

But just as I began to pull my leg back, I felt myself pushed roughly against a wall from behind. Caught off balance, I had no chance. I was pinned, a full weight against me. I could smell the glossy paint pressing against my nostrils.

I tried kicking backwards, hoping to land a blow on a shin, at least.

I heard a grunt as my heel hit what felt like a painful mix of flesh and bone. *Hit!*

"She kicking?" asked the NYC native.

"Yeah, little bitch got me," said his sidekick, sounding like he was talking about a mildly annoying mosquito bite. I clenched my fists but the guy's grip still held my wrists in a vice lock at my sides. He was pulling my arms halfway out of their sockets too. I tried to land another blow with one of my legs, but he'd stepped closer now and I didn't have the room to kick with any power. I squirmed my body hard, trying in vain to push his weight away.

"What do you *want* with me?" I screamed as I struggled. My cries echoed a little in the dark.

"Yelling won't help you in here! You really want to know what this is about?"

"Of course I do!" I wailed, pausing my flails so that I could hear his answer.

Rookie error. The moment I stilled my legs, the second guy pounced on both of my ankles. Wrapping his forearms around them, he yanked them up off the floor in one and the same move. One of my shoes fell off as my body twisted painfully to the horizontal and the guy behind me adjusted his grip and pulled my arms above my head.

Now they really had me. By the wrists and ankles, suspended in mid-air like a sack of potatoes. From there it was easy for them to lower me down onto the floor and hold me down with their weight again. One sat on my chest, squeezing most of the breath out of me, while the other kneeled further down my body, pinning my legs tight together with his thighs. I could wriggle no more.

"Okay, let's finish this job," said the lead guy.

What does that mean? My blood chilled.

I heard a brief clink of metal and then, powerless to move my ankles, felt something like a cuff snap shut around one of them. Then, inevitably, another. I could barely move a muscle in resistance.

"Okay, open the coat. And let's flip her over."

One tug of the belt and another twist of my body later, they had me where they wanted me. I was immobilized face down, wrists still bound, the skin of my naked breasts pressed to the hard, freezing floor. I gasped and shivered at its cold touch.

Working together, the duo was easily able to get my hands into a pair of cuffs as well. Like the ones on my feet, the chain between them was almost non-existent. Any useful movement was out of the question. They removed the special blurry glasses from my face. Not that it made any difference in this apocalyptic blackness. All my eyes could do in here was well up.

"Done. Now let's throw her in the elevator and get out of here."

I didn't know how much more of this I could take.

"Elevator?" I whimpered. "What? Where are you putting me now?"

The tears were finally flowing now. The taste of defeat felt like bile in my mouth.

"This elevator has only one destination," said the foreign-sounding guy, with a nasty kind of pleasure in his voice. I didn't like his tone one bit.

Both were on their feet now. Someone used a cellphone flashlight to find a button on the wall and hit it. Right away, I heard the unmistakable clunks of an elevator door sliding open. They really weren't kidding about sending me away.

There was no more light inside the elevator than there was in this entrance hallway, or wherever it was that we'd just been struggling. I was petrified to be put in there.

But there was absolutely nothing I could do to stop them dragging my half-naked body across the freezing floor and bundling me into the lift. They turned me onto my side and forced my knees to bend so I would fit inside. I could feel how claustrophobic the space was, even if I couldn't see it in the dark. Once in that fetal position, I had no chance to move out of it. Cuffed at both ends, I was trussed up like a hunter's catch.

As the door closed on me and my tiny, jet-black prison began to hurl itself upwards, there was nothing I could do but tremble with cold, terror and shame.

Chapter IX

Just a few seconds after taking off with its helpless, crumpled, dishevelled cargo, the elevator came to a halt once more. I hardly had time to concoct my worst-case scenario: that the door would open on a theatre stage. That the audience would be pointing and laughing.

And why shouldn't it happen? Whoever these people were that I was up against, they seemed to be creative.

Once the elevator had stilled, a soft, warm light came on inside the small space in which I was trapped. For the first time since I was taken from my home, I had both light and focus. Slowly eyes adjusted back to visual normality. I blinked as I took in the small mercy of sight. But if there was anything remarkable about the inside of the elevator, I didn't take it in. I was too desperate to know my fate.

This guesswork was the worst kind of torture. Apart from that first slap across the face I hadn't come to any physical harm so far, but if anything really terrible had to happen tonight, then I wanted it to happen soon. It might sound weird, but that's how I was thinking. Get it over with, let the deed be done, so I could go back to my life. Or to my grave, if that was the deal.

It felt like forever until the elevator door opened. And when it did, it seemed to do so in slow motion.

I'd been dumped diagonally across my mobile cage, pulled in feet first. With my head in one of the corners near the door, and unable to lift it while I was on my side with my limbs bound, I couldn't see what awaited me beyond it. I could only sense. Listen. Smell. Feel.

The first thing I picked up on as the door pulled back was warmth. It seeped into the musty elevator the moment it had a crack to crawl through. And more light, too. In those respects, at least, things were looking a lot better.

I also sensed human presence. And it felt familiar. Sharp as a razor blade.

"Laura."

I knew the voice.

The first syllable of my name dragged out, long and unhurried. The 'r' trilled by a practised tongue.

No! I was hallucinating again, wasn't I? That slap on the cheek had done more damage than I thought. Surely it couldn't be—

I held my breath as the owner of the voice stepped wordlessly inside the lift and gripped the right shoulder on which I was lying. I don't know how he was able to get a strong enough grip but with considerably more compassion than I'd gotten used to that night, he pulled my upper body off the floor. From there he was able to help me into a sitting position.

I was still facing towards the inside of the lift, and couldn't quite twist myself to see who it was towering over me. *He* had now taken a step back, prolonging my agony. Only when I glanced up did I realize that there was a mirror in the elevator.

I could only see the top half of my face in the mirror; I was too low down for anything else. And of that I was glad, given my current state. But I could see *him*.

Perfectly framed. Tommy.

No, really.

My jaw dropped wide open. My heart jumped into my throat as I blinked and blinked and blinked some more. I didn't know what to think. I wanted him to be my rescuer, not the latest man to attack my body and my dignity on this inexplicable night.

Could it be that he was here to save me? Had he somehow sent the two thugs packing and put this nightmare to an end? Wouldn't that be the slightly less outlandish explanation for why he was here? It was certainly the one I preferred.

But neither version seemed remotely plausible. The idea that Tommy would be part of a physical attack? It couldn't happen in real life — at least not in the world of suits and laptops and big money. Not here in the twenty-first century. It could only be a daydream. Was there something in that Prosecco I'd had at the wine bar?

It wasn't far-fetched to think he might be a figment of my imagination, was it? After all, I'd 'seen' him already today, as I'd sat at that window with a glass in my hand.

But the quality of my senses seemed too sharp this time. Nothing swam or shimmered or echoed like in a dream — and I was used to vivid ones, too. More than that, what I'd heard and what I'd seen matched up so perfectly well. Everything was unexpected and inappropriate and unacceptable, yes. But nothing seemed odd or inconsistent.

And if I was going to have fantasies about Tommy, wouldn't I have invented something far less harrowing than this?

I found my voice. And it was indignant.

"What in the *world* was that?"

He raised his eyebrows at me, prompting me to say something else in this weird mirror-conversation. Had I got it all wrong? Maybe he *was* my rescuer? Maybe this was a traditional Scottish business greeting, and I was being rude? Was it *me* who was the crazy one?

"That, Laura, was the capture of a beautiful woman," he replied, deadpan, looking directly at my eyes via the glass.

"*Capture?* I'm sorry, but is this a joke?"

I desperately hoped so. I felt like I needed more of an explanation before I could judge the situation. Or at least before I could calm the anger that was gradually replacing my fear. The ability to see, and with it the sight of a familiar face, was fast tipping the scales in favour of relieved rage. The fact was that I wasn't used to seeing people I met in broad daylight in my office as physical threats. Even though I didn't know this man, nor what he might be capable of.

Please be my rescuer.

Wait, had he just called me 'beautiful'? Suddenly I felt sick to the core. I knew what this was about! He wanted to seduce me into a compromising position. To force me into some kind of blackmail that would get the deal over the line. It was Andre's plan in reverse. He was going to use me as a pawn in his game, then drop me and laugh all the way to the bank. It was all falling into place.

He didn't reply to my question about the joke. He just stepped onto the lift threshold and scooped up my entire body. It was done in the classical style I had always associated with real gentlemen: one forearm under my knees and one supporting my back. I saw his eyes drop to my wide-open blouse. I blushed furiously and wriggled once more. It wasn't supposed to be like this. He was the pig behind all of this — wasn't he?

Fuck, I was confused.

"I want to inspect my prize," he murmured as he put me down on my feet in the middle of what appeared to be a plain foyer room. A grey carpet covered the floor while the walls were painted a deep, rich red. "Ah yes...still in your work clothes, I see. Or, at least, a few of them. Aye, it's a very pleasing state of affairs. Great look. I like dishevelled."

"*Prize?* What are you talking about? This is NOT funny!"

It didn't feel right to use his first name at this moment. So I used no name at all.

He responded by taking the two open sides of my blouse and coat and pulling both garments properly apart. They perched loose on my shoulders now, and any pretence at modesty was gone. Tommy could see everything I had: breasts, pussy and all that lay in between. My hands still cuffed behind my back, I could do nothing. Nothing but wait for his response.

"Kneel," he said. I just looked at him blankly. Kneel? On my knees?

In that moment I felt something like relief come over me. *Kneel?* That was so far down the rabbit hole, I felt sure it *had* to be a joke. A fucking long, weird one, sure, but a practical joke nonetheless. This couldn't be taken seriously. I'd obviously gotten it wrong in my head. A smile spread out across my face.

"All right, Tommy, you've had your fun. Your sense of humor is a bit different from ours, but okay, I've gone with it. No harm done. Is it time to have a drink now?"

I had to hand it to the beautiful Scotsman. This whole thing was way over the line, but part of me kind of liked the ending. One day, if he could script whatever happened next in such a way that it made sense, I might even forgive him.

Something in his face was supposed to have cracked by now. But instead of a hint of a smile or a twinkle in his eye, all I saw were deepening furrows in his brow. Unease swept over me like a squall across the sea. He let out a sharp, exasperated exhalation. It was like a cloud of anger was passing through his soul. He didn't look about to break into a belly laugh. Not one bit.

Instead, he lashed at me like a striking cobra. I didn't even see his hand moving before it struck my left breast. I reeled at the fury of the force.

"OW….FFFFFFFUCK!!" I yelled.

He'd landed his vicious bit of a slap square on my nipple. I'd never been hit there before. Never really considered that you *could* get hit there before. Shock waves ran from the centre of my breast and blasted right through my body like a quarry explosion. My brain went numb.

"I said *KNEEL!*"

I sank to my knees without a word.

My smile was wiped clean off my face. My body was now shaking with horror and panic.

Chapter X

Over the next thirty-six hours or so, it became abundantly clear that this thing that was happening to me was neither a game nor a dream nor the result of a dud batch of Prosecco. Twisted and warped it may have been — but it was reality.

Tommy had been straight-faced when he'd made me kneel and explained to me that I was now 'his'. That I would be 'used for his gratification' and that I wouldn't be going back to work 'for a while'. That if I ever talked back again, I could expect a far more protracted response than a slap on the breast. I'd looked up into his battleship-grey eyes for one last hint that his face was about to break, but they flashed with nothing but powerful disquiet. Tommy did not do practical jokes.

I'd wanted to ask so much. Where was this *really* going? If he wanted to seduce me and then use ensuing events against me and Kerstein, then why not be nice about it? He *must* have known that he didn't need to anything like mastermind a kidnapping to get me where he wanted me.

No, it couldn't be about him luring me into a sexual web that would come back to bite me later. This capture business had to have something to do with the deal he and Danscombe wanted, but I dismissed the talk of 'a beautiful woman' as some kind of front. Tommy had only known me since that morning, and then only as Kerstein's legal chief — how could this kidnapping be anything other than strictly business?

And then, did he seriously have London's backing for this psychotic performance, or was it simply his own strategy? Was he trying to send a particular message to Kerstein? Was this about ransom? How could he be so blatantly criminal and hope to get away with it?

Even the questions were crazy.

But I'd not dared ask anything more of him on that first night. Apart from the sheer shock, I had learnt that Tommy could hurt me at any time he chose. I'd already seen how quickly he could lash out. First in the entrance hallway, and then after he moved me into what he weirdly referred to as my 'display cabinet'.

I'd spent every moment in that room since he'd hauled me up off my knees in front of the elevator, thrown me over his shoulder like a bag of carrots and carried me through what seemed remarkably like an empty office building. From what I'd been able to see as my head dangled impotently at his back, my nose knocking against the grey material of the blazer he wore, it wasn't the kind of place anybody lived. It definitely had the air of an office, but one mostly devoid of furniture and features. I saw no people as we crossed the floor.

By the time we'd gotten from the elevator to my 'display cabinet', I felt sure this had once been a place where people worked. But that those people had cleared out — from this floor, at least.

Since then, I had kept on returning to those same questions. My mind had been broiling with them.

Kidnapped? Really? Okay, Tommy hadn't used that word, but it's how I actually interpreted his talk of 'taking' me.

Kidnapped by a business counterpart. One whom I'd met for the first time only that day, in a classy, minimalist conference room. A respectable, educated person who worked for a multinational company. A company with lawyers and a reputation. I couldn't get my brain to add those realities together and come up with what was happening to me now. The base criminality. It *didn't* add up.

And yet, Tommy had most certainly dumped me in this little glass-fronted room and locked me inside. And the savage had already begun to show me what he could do to me if I crossed him.

My quarters, if that was the right word, had clearly once been a corner office, of the sort senior managers in big companies all over the world occupy. A reasonably spacious rectangle, it measured perhaps 15 feet by 20. One of the long sides was solid and one of the short ones mostly window. Of the two interior walls, one was plain and the other was completely transparent.

This see-through wall commanded a view over part of the open-plan area. There was very little of interest out there. It was just a sad space: the odd forgotten swivel-chair, a few surviving cubicle dividers and, here and there, the black snake of an electric cable slithering across the floor. I had a panorama of abandonment — and that was quite fitting.

No lights came on at night. All I could make out in the expanse out there was the spooky silhouettes of that lonely office debris.

The decor in my prison was identical to that I'd seen outside the elevator: rhinoceros-grey carpet, blood-red walls and snow-white ceiling. The carpet was softer underfoot though. It was actually one of those squishy ones that are a nightmare to clean but a delight to walk on in stockings. This part wasn't very managerial at all. It couldn't have been like that originally.

As for walking on the carpet in stockings, that was wishful thinking. I was already down to one shoe when I arrived in the elevator, thanks to my struggle with the thugs downstairs. Once Tommy had brought me into this room, with some kind of high-tech door having closed itself safely behind him, he'd produced a key from his pocket and removed the ankle and wrist cuffs. He'd made me stand in front of him and take off the shoe. Then my coat. My blouse. And finally my tights. I was down to zero clothing. I would only walk this carpet barefoot.

Still reeling from my reception outside the lift, I had blindly obeyed him. I'd meekly handed him each and every item, one by one, straight after I removed it. There had been nothing to stop me kicking him in the balls before I took off that shoe. He was right there, directly in front of me. But even if I could have stunned him for a moment, I knew I wouldn't be able to work that door. I would only succeed in angering him more, and that would end badly for me.

More than that, I was shocked into submission. I still couldn't take on board the fact that any of this was happening. I was back to thinking it was too far-fetched to be anything other than a wicked combination of hallucination and nightmare. And since it couldn't be real, trying to strike back at my captor didn't really make sense. Especially since the pain I'd felt in this had *actually* hurt — imaginary or otherwise. I didn't want to provoke any more of that.

So I'd done exactly as I was told when he'd impatiently made me strip off each last item of clothing until I was completely naked. And since Tommy had taken those clothes away with him, that's how I'd remained ever since.

A thin, single mattress, barely any improvement on the carpet, was laid out on the floor, its head to the centre of the solid wall at the back of the room. It was the only place I could even pretend to try and rest. But when you had to lie down naked, with no blanket and no pillow, wondering if a crowd of people might flood into the deserted open-plan outside and then start to ogle you, it just didn't work. If round-the-clock torture had been the plan for me, then it was working well: even trying to sleep was nothing but a prolonged, one-eye-open agony.

The most suffocating torment, though, was the sense that I was being watched remotely. Well, maybe. And perhaps only sometimes. I had only my imagination to go on — but there was plenty for it to work with.

First, there were cameras on me. These were mounted high up in each corner of the room, their beady eyes trained my way all the time. Sometimes I could hear them moving, with their little electric groans. Whether someone was operating them or they shifted automatically, I didn't know. But it was sinister as a snake.

Then there was the bewitching monitor mounted on the transparent wall at the front of the room.

It was about four feet wide and three feet high, similar in shape to a top-of-the-range television. But it was framed more like a window, and it had a life of its own. Sometimes it was just 'off', looking pretty much like you'd expect one-way glass to look. Other times it glowed the colour of the sun, or purple, or luminescent green. It turned out to be the only light source in the room. Sometimes it would suddenly brighten the office in the middle of the night, as if to remind me that there was not one tiny thing I could control in this place.

"I can watch you through there, if I feel like it," was one of the few things Tommy had said to me when he'd 'settled me in'. "Make sure you're being a good girl. And you won't know whether I'm there or not — so you'd better be a good girl all the time."

What the *fuck* was he talking about? Did he think I was his daughter?

I hadn't answered, of course. I didn't tell him to fuck off and I didn't hit him — both of which I really wanted to do — but actually acknowledging him was something I couldn't summon up the strength to do either. And that had been a bad idea. The second time in a matter of minutes that I'd pushed him into a reaction.

He'd clamped one of his long-fingered hands around my throat and twisted my nipple so hard I thought it would come clean off my breast. The pain filled my eyes with tears.

"You will *answer* me, Laura," he'd growled, revealing just how well his accent could lend itself to aggression. "And you will do so with utmost respect. Trust me, this is just a hint of what I will do to you."

I wasn't clear if that 'will' only applied to situations where I didn't answer him. Or if it was something he was going to do anyway. But I had certainly understood that displeasing him was both easy to do and ill-advised. But I'd nodded with a whimper and croaked out a 'yes'.

"Better," he'd said, giving my nipple an extra final twist that made me yelp, then letting go of my throat as well. I'd panted heavily, the air in the room thick with tension.

Whatever air *did* exist in the room was of the artificial variety. Unusually for a prison (I supposed), there was that large window. But there was no way to open it, of course. And you wouldn't want to, anyway, since we appeared to be several floors up. The view was actually amazing. Like something you'd expect from a fancy hotel suite. I could catch glimpses of the Hudson River, and, quite eerily, I could clearly see the Kerstein building from here. I wasn't entirely convinced that one of the top-floor windows in view wasn't the boardroom where our negotiations always took place. The place where I'd met my abductor just hours before...*this*.

But that window was a torture in its own way. Though I was high up, other windows on other buildings were higher still. It was a busy skyline — this was NYC, after all. Thank God we weren't directly opposite a building with windows at the same height. It wasn't like people could look in on me during their smoke breaks. But what if window-cleaners came to *this* building? And what if someone had binoculars?

I felt reasonably safe in the daytime, and the view even provided me with a lift of sorts. But at night, if the bright lights came on through the screen, I felt brutally exposed.

I loathed this shame I felt. I knew I should *want* someone to be able to see me. If I wanted to get rescued, then somebody had to see there was a prisoner behind *that* window on *that* floor, on *that* street. That's how rescues worked! But the shyness I felt for my naked body trumped everything. Only now did I truly understand (and curse) how deep the awful, painful perception of my own body ran. It had played its part in getting me into this mess.

But anyway, if someone were to see me, they'd probably just think I was a kinky exhibitionist, wouldn't they? Who else sits around naked in front of a big window, with all the lights on?

There was a thing worse than that window, though. Whoever could see me — outside, via camera or through that eerie screen — would also be able to watch me use the toilet in the corner.

Yes, somebody had gone to the trouble of fitting a flush toilet here. You didn't find *that* next to your boss's desk, that was for sure. It had to have been put there for the specific purpose of...prisoners. People like me.

The toilet was clean and it flushed, but of course there was nowhere to hide when I used it. Not even a little curtain. I could think of no higher humiliation. Especially when I never knew if I *was* being watched. By some Scottish sicko — and maybe even his buddies too. Maybe even by every sordid webcam fan looking for jerk-off material on the internet. Just that I *might* be.

I couldn't move the little mattress away from its position right in front of the screen, either. It was fixed in place on the carpet. Of course it was.

This repurposed office truly was, in every sense, a display cabinet. And that, apart from a tiny sink next to the toilet where I could scoop up a drink of water with my hand, was just about all you could say about the little room that held me captive.

I hardly even looked at the door. It was some fancy electronic thing. It had no handle. The middle was of a dark, opaque, glass-like material, the frame of matte metal. Both looked uncompromisingly strong. The door seemed to be controlled by fingerprint recognition, or something like that. When he had brought me here, Tommy had just given the electronic surface of the door itself a light touch. And with that, it had opened up for him.

Anyway, I couldn't quite reach the door. Because I was chained. Once Tommy had finished making me strip on arrival, he had put an iron shackle around my left ankle, which was secured to the wall next to the mattress by a heavy, old-fashioned chain. The last link at each end of the chain was kept in place by equally no-nonsense padlocks, which offered no hope of manipulation whatsoever.

There was plenty of slack in the chain. But not enough to start thinking about shoulder-charging my way through the glass (it probably wasn't real glass, but who the fuck knew what those transparent office walls were made of?) or any other bullish escape plans. I could get up to the observation screen (though my instinct was to do the exact opposite) but couldn't get to the front wall on the diagonal. This ruled out the door, which was in the corner.

I could get a couple of yards from the window, but no nearer. Even to use the toilet was tight. I kind of had to leave my left leg behind, stuck out at a crazy angle. Nice for *someone*, I guessed.

And food? Nothing. Not a crumb for the first two nights. But I barely noticed. I wasn't feeling hungry at all. It felt like my body had been shocked into shutdown.

What had I done to deserve this? Being treated like a zoo animal, only without feeding time? I could *not* believe that I'd been attracted to this man. How wrong we can be. How spectacularly, disastrously wrong.

Chapter XI

After two nights and a day of this, Wednesday morning arrived. It was as bright, blue and sunny as the morning Tommy had walked into our office for the first time. It felt like weeks ago now, much less the start of this one. Time does strange things when you're imprisoned.

Now that Tommy's first tasters of violence were no longer so fresh in my mind, I simply sat and seethed. How could this be happening to me on a beautiful spring day in the middle of New York City? It still didn't seem real. But when I began to feel hunger knocking at my stomach for the first time, I knew it had to be.

The kidnapping played out in my mind, over and over. How could I have stopped those two men, whom I assumed Tommy had engaged to do the dirty work he didn't want to risk in public? Did I leave the front door unlocked, or had they somehow broken in earlier on, through the kitchen perhaps? Could I have fought harder? And how *dumb* had I been to worry about being exposed — ridiculous! I could have run away from my captors at any time, couldn't I?

They'd totally played me. They wouldn't really have opened up my coat on a busy street!

What if I had just stayed at work like a grown-up? *None of this would have happened.* Or would it? I still didn't have even the faintest theory about why I'd been taken by the man from our major client. I could have bought into the seduction idea, but the violent capture, imprisonment and treatment made no sense. I even began to wonder if I had said something offensive to him on that first morning.

The idea of having upset him seemed ridiculous — we'd barely spoken, and though the thought made me frown darkly now, I'd been smitten by him. And anyway, even if I had caused some offence, what kind of psycho *kidnaps* a woman just because she bruised his ego?

The idea of some sort of deal-making tool was pure fiction too. You don't win negotiations by committing major crimes, do you? That's called dirt, and it usually works strongly in favour of your counterpart. Anyway, I didn't see that Tommy was getting anything much by keeping me here right now. Where was the benefit?

I had way too much time to think. The real jail cell wasn't those four walls, but inside my head. I had nothing to do but beat myself up. I couldn't even see the beginnings of an idea of how to escape.

Crawling nearer to the window to get a break from my thoughts and look at the outside world — my one saving grace in this little hutch — became a daytime habit. I felt safer and less embarrassed that way. It would be harder for anybody to see me if I kept low. And if they did, they would see less of me.

With every window visit I grew more and more certain that I could see the Kerstein office. I knew it might be my imagination; some product of my longing for a connection to the outside world. But how could I help thinking about what they were thinking over there? I'd disappeared for an afternoon, then missed a full day's work. Now I was AWOL well into a second morning, and still they hadn't heard a word from me.

If someone disappears from the office, and doesn't even call in sick, people are going to think that person has had a terrible accident. I doubted Andre would care very much (apart from insofar as it interfered with his plans for me to catch Tommy in some sticky romantic web), but maybe Human Resources would try to get in touch with my family. And if that didn't work, surely the police would get a call too.

But the cops had nothing obvious to go on: no crashed cars, no mangled patient lying in a hospital, no crime scene on the street. Then again, they might be able to pick up a trail from my house. I tried to think if any clues might have been left behind when my assailants had forced themselves on me. Surely some buttons on the floor? My bra?

They'd conclude that I'd been in some kind of sexually-fuelled situation. The thought embarrassed me. *Jesus, Laura! Embarrassed? Really?* Nothing very sexual had even happened! In a way, the clues would be misleading.

Maybe the attackers had gone back to the house, gotten inside by whatever means they used the first time around, and cleared up any traces of the struggle. But even if they'd gone to such trouble, surely I must have passed dozens of CCTV cameras (the good kind) as they'd led me across town? That went for the hours before my capture, too: perhaps the police had already traced my movements to the wine bar in which I'd spent the afternoon, and had interviewed that cute waiter.

Then again, maybe they hadn't even registered me as missing yet. Don't they wait 72 hours or something? I sighed. Not knowing was just as horrible as not being able to do anything.

Kneeling miserably at the window, my eye returned to that office building of mine and my thoughts returned to work. What was happening with the negotiations? What had Tommy said, or not said? Were he and Andre squaring up in the conference room at this very moment? Or was Tommy on the other side of that inky screen-thing, watching me? Maybe he had disappeared on Kerstein too?

I thought about emails I'd been supposed to reply to and reports whose deadlines I'd missed. Then I beat myself up for thinking about them. *You're imprisoned, for fuck's sake! Kidnapped!*

My lack of perspective hit me like cold sleet. It was becoming clear just how deep my work sickness ran. How out of whack my priorities had become. But those work thoughts were only fleeting. If one thing hadn't changed since Monday morning, it was that I still didn't want to be in the office. Surprisingly, maybe, no part of me was pining to be at work. Trotting hurriedly around that big, flashy building with a coffee in my hand or hacking insanely away at my keyboard was better than being chained up, naked and humiliated — obviously — but something in between, like grabbing a free bubbly at my neighbourhood wine bar, seemed a great option now.

Suddenly the little things I'd stopped giving myself time for became the big things I craved. Everything I'd been taking for granted while I worked myself stupid and tried to forget my status as a cheated-on divorcee. I wanted to be sitting down on a cushy sofa with a book. I wanted to be taking a soothing soak in a bubble bath. I missed my favourite wine glasses. I longed to look out onto my little yard behind the kitchen window. Hell, even reading the newspaper on the rattling, air-starved subway would be like a dream come true right now.

Was I just giving myself little mirages to hold onto in this awful situation? Maybe. But I had to keep my brain occupied. It was used to ticking over all day long. It was even used to ticking over at night, spinning those wild dreams for me. But, of course, I hadn't slept a wink in this place yet. I would have to be way more exhausted before I would be able to let myself go in this fishbowl.

One time, the thought hit me that he was making a non-stop, *Big Brother*-style film of me. A live camera of a totally naked woman kept prisoner in some sort of abandoned office building. My blood froze as I thought about what sort of hits that might get on the internet. There had to be sickos out there who'd be into that sort of thing. Probably Tommy was one of them. Maybe that was his *real* business.

I tried not to think about this storyline too much. It seemed as plausible as any other explanation for this madness, and I didn't like that one bit.

It wasn't particularly cold in my cell — at least not yet — but I shivered when I thought about my parents or my kids finding out about my current plight via a webcam link. And then, once I'd finished thinking how stupid it was to crave anything other than being found by any means possible, I would start to miss them terribly.

I hated the thought that they'd probably been informed of my disappearance and were worried sick right now. And that there was nothing whatsoever I could do to ease their minds. I could deal with my own suffering, but I loathed myself for not being able to get them a message. The thought of it made me well up just about every hour.

It wasn't like me to get emotional about family like that. But, locked away in this lonely room, I pined for the very connection that I'd been shying away from when I was free. I'd made very little effort to see my immediate family, and that had been a voluntary (if not exactly conscious) decision. Now that my freedom had been taken, and I knew I couldn't just call up Harriet or my mother, I longed to spend time with them.

Maybe it was just the thought that I would never see them again. I had no idea if I was going to survive this. What did Tommy plan for me? He'd shown already that he wouldn't shy away from a low level of violence. Would he...*kill me?*

Whatever kind of kidnapping this was, and whatever mysterious motives I was dealing with, murder seemed too dramatic, too far-fetched. It belonged in Hollywood. *But you'd have said that about kidnapping too!* This crazy caging was already messing with what I saw as believable or otherwise.

I began to long for a visit from Tommy. Sure, I wanted to give him a piece of my mind. After so much time alone in here since his first round of abuse, I had no idea how exactly I would react to him. But more than anything, I wanted some answers. I wanted to know what was going to happen to me. Or what had to happen for this thing to end.

Because one thing was for sure: it couldn't go on like this indefinitely. There had to be some plan. I thirsted for answers.

By the time Tommy finally walked in on what felt like the latter part of the second morning — I had no way of telling the actual time — I was ready to take answers over both clothing and food. That's how badly I needed to make sense of things.

I was lying on my thin mat, resting my eyes if not my brain, when he came back. I became aware of a sound in the far corner of the room. It was the light click of the door unlocking, then the gentle electronic whirr of its opening inwards towards me.

Curled up on my side, in the most modest position I had been able to come up with, I instinctively curled up even tighter when I opened my eyes and saw him towering just inside the entrance. In that moment my vulnerability hit home hard. This time my fight mechanism kicked in, and my rage poured out.

"What the *fuck* do you think you're doing?" I blurted out. I was screaming louder than I'd ever screamed. My lungs hadn't worked that hard since I was a small child who'd spilled her milk. I *wanted* someone to hear me. "Let me go and get the *fuck* out my country!!"

When I'd pictured how this might go, I'd imagined calmly teasing the information I needed out of my captor. Winning a calculated victory with tact and guile. Clearly that plan had gone somewhat astray at the very outset.

Tommy began to stride towards me, his eyes flashing with an anger just like my own. They were on fire and his urgent footsteps shook the floor.

"WHAT DO YOU WANT FROM ME??!!"

I was pushing now, and I knew it. I'd been unaware just how much uncontrollable anger had been swelling inside me since I'd been stuck in this room.

"Get AWAY from—"

I had no chance to finish that sentence. His hand was already clamped tight over my mouth. It wrenched my head sideways, twisting my neck into a contorted, painful position as I tried to stay on my right shoulder and somehow shield my body from him.

He'd moved behind me and was down on one knee. His thigh pressed against my back. I could smell his cologne. I began to shake.

"You will choose your words far more carefully from now on, young lady," he said, sounding far more calm than his body language had been.

Young? Are you kidding me? I'm at least a few years older than you, you prick.

I tried to say it out loud, but all I could produce was muffled mumbles. I could taste the tang of perspiration on his palm as it squashed my lips into wordlessness. I tried to bite his hand, but the pressure was too much for me to move.

"I thought you might have decided to be a good girl in this time you've been alone," he continued, with the same unnerving, tranquil authority. "But it looks like I'm going to have to show you some good reasons to behave."

Behave? There he went again. Whatever his delusion was, I could see one silver lining. He wasn't planning to kill me. Only the living can behave.

"You can scream all you want in here. Nobody will hear you. But I will *not* stand for such conduct. You'll respect me if you know what's good for you. *Understand?*"

I didn't understand. I didn't understand the tiniest part of any of this. Feeling overpowered and helpless once again, I began to whimper.

"If you'll calm yourself, I'll let you speak," he offered.

I nodded, choking both from the tears and the half-portions of air I was getting. I just wanted to be let go from this position. I would still be chained, but at least I could shift my body. Freedom is a relative concept.

My steam had been thoroughly blown off for now. I felt so defeated that I was ready to return to my strategy of reasonable engagement.

He ripped his hand away from my mouth. I could feel him stand up behind me.

"Now kneel," he said. His tone was an odd mix of patience and boredom.

God, we were back to that kneeling thing. I sighed, then tensed with fear at the thought that he might have heard the frustrated exhalation. *Just do it, Laura. Play along for the moment. You need to know what you're dealing with.*

I hesitated, unable to bring myself to simply leap up and do as he said. Then, as slowly as I thought I might get away with, I rolled clumsily onto my front, pushed my torso up with my hands and tucked my knees and ankles underneath me. I instinctively knew I had to face him. I was eye-level with the crotch of his grey suit trousers. He was about two feet in front of me, looming up like the Empire State Building. I could feel the cool of my metal ankle-shackle against my bare butt cheek.

"That's a good start," he said. "Every time I come in here, you'll kneel just like that on your mat. Immediately. Unless you're told otherwise."

I could feel the rebellion rise through my body and crash through to every corner of my soul. But I held my tongue. *Just for now.*

"Okay," I said in a near-whisper. I might have decided to cooperate, but I wasn't going to respond to this fucking criminal military-style. "Will you please tell me what you want with me now? I'm lost. Is this some kind of negotiating tactic?"

I just stopped myself from putting a 'sick' in front of 'negotiating tactic'. I was hoping for some progress here. I had to stick to my guns.

Tommy looked thrown for just a moment.

"I beg your pardon?"

"I mean, I assume this is some sort of kidnapping in order to get the deal you want for Danscombe? I can't think of any other reason why you would do this."

His mouth twitched. Then it turned into the kind of smile you don't necessarily think is going to lead to good things. He chuckled.

"Oh, I see. You think this is about business?"

I nodded. Already his reaction was puzzling me.

"I'm amused that you think that, Laura. You think I need to take prisoners in order to do my job?"

I shrugged. "I don't know. I really don't. What else am I supposed to think? Why else would you capture someone you just met?"

He drew in a deep breath and gazed over towards the window. I looked up at him. I could see the tough sinews of his neck tighten as his face turned away from me. A few seconds passed. I waited.

"You don't need to know everything," he said, his attention seemingly on a spot somewhere well beyond the Hudson. "It's high time you learnt some trust, in fact."

Who the *fuck* did he think he was, giving me a moral lecture like I was some kind of out-of-line schoolgirl? Christ, this diplomacy game was getting sorely tested already.

"I don't need to know everything, you're right," I said, my heart beating wildly. "But the reason why I've been wrenched away from my life and taken prisoner...I think anybody would want to know that."

He turned his face back to me. I brought my eyes down, looking instead at the V where his trouser legs came together. I had no idea if that was the right thing to do in this situation.

I pushed on, wanting to make some kind of impact before I lost my nerve.

"It sounds like you're not planning on killing me. And if it's not about the deal, then…"

I trailed off. I didn't want to follow that thought to its natural conclusion, which had all sorts of unpleasantness about it. There were some images I definitely didn't need to put into my head. Far better for them to stay on the periphery.

"I didn't say it wasn't about the deal, did I?"

I wondered if I had missed something. Hadn't he just said it wasn't about business?

"Oh, but I thought—"

"What I *said*, Laura," he interrupted, "was that I don't *need* to take prisoners in order to do my job."

"Well, yes...so…I'm confused…"

He bent at the waist, bringing his eyes down to mine. Still he had to tilt his head towards me, such was his height. I could see the strong and perfectly straight line of his nose, pointing towards me like a soldier's arrow.

"Sometimes we do things we don't need to do, Laura. And I, in particular, often do things I *want* to do."

The urge to plant a slap on that cheek of his was almost irresistible. Why was I having this ludicrous Mad Hatter conversation with this caveman? But I stayed my hand. Patience would be my watchword.

"All right then," I said, "So is there anything you can tell me?"

"You'll find things out by doing and experiencing, Laura. Not by being told. That's not my style. All I will repeat for now is that if you do as you're told and cooperate, things will work out for you."

I sighed. This wasn't getting me anywhere. Clearly Tommy enjoyed being Mr Evasive. This was all a game to him. My eyes sank to a point on the grey, carpeted floor somewhere behind Tommy's knee. My mind was going numb already, and I felt bound in more ways than one. Was this resignation? So soon?

Before I could argue with myself any further, Tommy stood up straight once more, reached into his right pocket and took something out. Curious, I couldn't help glancing up at it.

"Recognize this, Laura?"

My phone!!

There was no doubting it. The cover had a picture of a leaping killer whale on it, with a little crack running diagonally across the top half of the plastic. Definitely mine. Tommy's crooks must have grabbed it from the table downstairs where I always dumped my stuff when I came into the house.

Seeing my property in his hand incensed me. It made the sheer criminality of this whole thing hit home harder. Instinctively, I shot out my left hand to try and grab it.

I wasn't nearly quick enough. Tommy was fast as a cat. He caught my wrist with his free hand, twisting the skin so hard it felt like carpet burn.

While I winced and yelped, Tommy growled a fierce whisper at me.

"Do you think that's the kind of behaviour I was referring to when I mentioned 'cooperation'?"

I refused to answer, biting my lip and looking towards the door instead. But it was a hopeless game.

"Oh, that was a *very* bad move, Laura."

Like a flash he adjusted his grip on me, moving it from my wrist to the base of my second and third fingers before I could react. Then, still with my phone in his other hand, he sprung around behind me and shoved my hand towards my mouth.

"OPEN IT!"

For the first time since I'd been brought to this room, I was truly terrified. I could smell and taste Tommy's rage, and suddenly testing him seemed a very bad idea. I did as he told me, opening my jaw.

He barely waited for me to part my lips before he plunged those two fingers straight inside. My tongue dived out of the way like a coward, and a fraction of a second later Tommy had rammed my own fingers straight into my throat. I gagged immediately, coughing and blubbing as my body lurched at the shock.

He pulled back slightly for a moment, then made me attack my own throat again. And again and again. I was gasping and choking. Deep-throating my own fingers. His knuckles contorted my cheeks as they held my own knuckles where he wanted them. I began drooling over both our hands as he continued to hammer with no regard for anything but my pain and humiliation.

"Don't *try* me, Laura. Just *DON'T!*"

He'd stopped for a second to tell me this, holding my fingers just on the edge of the gag zone. My lawyer brain scrambled to stay rational, taking snapshots and notes for the trial he was going to have to face if I came out of this alive.

Chapter XII

Just when I thought I couldn't gag another time without passing out, Tommy pulled my spit-soaked fingers out of my throat and threw my limp, quivering hand to the floor with such force that my weakened, shaking body toppled over.

I crumpled into a gasping heap on the mat. My knees were still curled and my left arm extended pathetically across the floor like some D-grade ballerina trying to fold herself away into a convincing final pose. Only once in my life had I experienced something like that. It had been with a slightly older German guy, after dark on a beach during that same trip to Asia. It had been something other than my own fingers, of course — but it hadn't been anything like as intense as this.

That attack on my curious and youthful throat was an eternity ago. George would never have tried something like that, of course. Such scenes were a possibility I had forgotten about.

All I wanted was to be left alone there for a moment and gather my senses. But instead I tried to wriggle back upright into that kneeling position, worried that I'd be in more trouble if I failed to do so. But my head went light as I tried to lift my torso, and I got no further than propping myself onto my forearms, like a Sphinx gone wrong.

Tommy knew I was defeated. I could feel a roughness on the back of my throat, like he'd actually bruised me there. It would have been one thing if he'd done it with his own fingers, but to manipulate mine into self-abuse? That made me feel wretched.

I was so demoralized and disorientated that I didn't even care that the most intimate parts of my body must have been on clear display to my tormentor behind me. Not that Tommy seemed to have much interest in that. I could hear him getting up to his feet, then his footsteps taking him casually over towards the window.

"So now, Laura," he said after a deep breath, "I hope I won't have to be doing that again before we make some progress today."

He spoke so casually and calmly. Nothing in his voice told of a man who had been half-choking somebody just seconds ago. I could see how it happened that I kept on underestimating the threat he posed. You just couldn't imagine him pouncing on you — and then he would do exactly that. How could I possibly fight such cold-blooded, clinical brutality?

I tried to scrape my wits together, still panting heavily. I couldn't get up to look at him. Well, maybe I could have, but now some instinct wanted him to see my suffering. To know what pain he had inflicted. To witness the bout of sickly coughs that now seized me. It seemed like my only hope would be for some sympathy to awaken deep inside him.

Not that my conscious brain could possibly imagine where sympathy might be hiding inside such a monstrous human being.

When I finally managed to bring the coughing fit under control, I summoned up enough strength to shake my head in response to his statement and murmur a weak 'no'. Now, I supposed I would find out what he meant by 'progress'.

"Good," he continued. "Because we're going to let your family know they don't have to worry about you. Or rather, *you're* going to let them know. Much more convincing, I always think. I assume you'd like them to know you're alive?"

There were many ways I could have chosen to answer this little speech. All of them were bitter and sarcastic. But if he was going to boil it down into a yes or no question, then clearly there was only one answer.

I took a deep breath through my nose and swallowed hard. It hurt.

"Yes," I croaked, my forehead still buried on my forearms.

"Then I need your passcode."

Oh yes, I almost forgot. He had my phone. That's why I'd ended up in this wheezing, forlorn mess.

I had nothing left in the tank right now. No way could I take more violence. My only option was to give him what he wanted.

"One. Six. Six. Two."

A moment went by while he tapped the screen. My heart leapt with fear and my senses began to awaken as the stark reality of my kidnapper now having access to my phone became apparent.

"Good girl, we're in. See how easy that could have been? Now I'll just have a little read. Need to get into the role a bit, you know?"

The room went quiet as Tommy scrolled through my phone and seemed to forget about me. Driven by the irrational idea that being able to see what he was doing could make any difference to his plans for the rest of this visit, I forced myself up off the floor.

Well, at least as far as a kneeling position. I couldn't forget that part. I was now thoroughly petrified of angering him again. The pain of swallowing through my dry throat was a constant reminder of what could happen if I did. I was desperate for a drink of water, but I dared not go for the tap right now.

He said nothing for several minutes. Occasionally he chuckled. *What's he reading this time?* I racked my brains to try to think of what embarrassing things might be on my phone, but I couldn't come up with much. Thank God, I wasn't the sort of person to be taking compromising selfies or downloading flirting apps. Nor was I the sort of person to text girlfriends about the tall, handsome Scottish guy who'd just become a part of my life at the office.

Once upon a time that might have been me. When I was younger, every little spark or drama captivated me. I cared about who looked at me and how. I cared about who'd done what with whom. I cared about my tan and getting compliments. I was even a jealous bitch now and then. But it was a few years since I'd been bothered with all of that. I'd been married — and vaguely content enough not to sniff around.

As for exchanging gossip, I didn't really have any partners in crime for that. I'd been busy enough during the last few years to alienate most of the girlfriends I'd had in my thirties. Just as work had taken over my life, I suspected it had largely taken over my phone. I wasn't much worried that Tommy was going to find anything that would make me blush.

"Quite distant with your family, aren't you?" Tommy said at last. "It's not going to be much of a challenge to sound like you in a text message to Harriet or your parents, is it? You just say what you need to say, and that's it."

I wasn't sure if that required an answer. One thing was for sure, he'd found out certain things well before his fingers started dancing on my touchscreen just now.

"You...you know my kids' names?"

"Harriet and Luke, yes. I know a lot about you, as a matter of fact."

I paused, wanting to know more.

"But how have you found out so much when you've only been here for a couple of days? How did you plan...this?"

I hoped desperately that I was injecting enough fawning admiration into my tone that these questions wouldn't upset him and his 'you don't need to know everything' idea.

"Who said I just stepped off the plane on Monday morning?"

Nobody had. I guess I'd assumed too much.

"So you've been around in New York for a while?"

"In a roundabout sort of way," he said, reverting to non-specific answers. "I travel a lot. I do a lot of different things."

I frowned. How long had he been stalking me? And how? And didn't his work with Danscombe keep him busy enough?

"Be quiet now," he ordered. "I'm composing a message to your daughter."

He paced the room in front of me, striding back and forth as his thumbs danced across my touch-screen. I supposed he was going to write something that would explain my disappearance without causing alarm. Not that my kids would have noticed I was missing, unless they'd tried to spontaneously visit. Which didn't happen very often at all.

"Excellent," he said, making a decisive final press with his thumb. "Message sent. Like I said, you're not very hard to imitate. Now I want you to read your handiwork."

He came over to me again, bending down just as he had before the latest attack. He held the phone up before my eyes, barely twelve inches away. I could feel his breath.

That cellphone was totally within grabbing distance. But Tommy seemed totally confident I wasn't going to grab it. And on that score he was one hundred percent correct.

He was showing me the familiar interface of the chat history I had with my daughter. Even on this one screen, the dates stretched back to February. We didn't message much. I guess we saw each other *just* often enough that we didn't really have to.

The latest message, bearing my name, read as follows.

Just letting you know that I've gone away for a while. We've taken the negotiations to London, so basing myself there for a few weeks. Not sure how long it will take, but I guess it won't be as quick as I would like. Take care!

The further I read, the faster I began to breathe. I felt the air race through my nostrils as I snatched one stupidly small ration of air after the next. My brain was already kicking into the implications of what I was seeing, and now my lungs were racing to keep up with my galloping fears.

It was a perfectly innocent and reasonable message. Harriet would think nothing of it. After all, the communication came directly from me. How could she possibly know that 'Mom' was in fact naked and chained, locked in a deserted office high up in some Manhattan tower? That those words from 'Mom' were in fact the work of a hulk of a man with a weird accent?

She wouldn't hear the masculine voice. She wouldn't smell his manly scent. She wouldn't know how big the thumbs that typed that message really were. All she would see would be those blank-faced letters on her screen: 'Mom.'

And she'd think Mom was just fine.

I felt a new wave of panic well up inside me. Seeing that message in front of my eyes left no room for doubt. Tommy would stop at nothing to make sure my disappearance wouldn't be noted by anybody as such. He would work everything out just as smartly as those two men — the attackers who'd played me into walking here so dumbly — had done.

"Your mother and your son will be receiving similar messages," announced Tommy, straightening up and folding his arms. The phone was out of my reach now. *You should have grabbed it!*

Every rebellious impulse that entered my brain seemed to be like that: child's play once the moment was gone.

"And what happens when — "

I stopped myself. I was about to give away my one and only lifeline. Why did I open my mouth?

"Yes?"

Tommy looked distinctly interested in what I had been about to say. How could I back out?

"What happens when...too much time has gone by?"

It was a quick-fix. One I prayed would work. I knew he could force my real question out of me if he suspected I'd changed it.

He didn't, thank God.

"By the time 'too much time' has gone by, Laura, you won't need me to send messages for you. Trust me on that."

More fucking ambiguity. But at least he hadn't prised out the crucial piece of information I'd almost blurted out. And that was the fact that my kids had keys to my house. And that every now and then, they dropped by and stayed a night or two.

Maybe those hoodlums had gone back to the place and tidied it up, just in case. Probably they did. But what if they'd left something out of place? What if they'd missed a piece of the puzzle? A tiny giveaway that wouldn't look quite right?

That was a big 'if'. And even then, deep down, I had major doubts about my kids' ability to notice some small clue that might alert them. *I* would pick up on a stray bra or a front door that hadn't been locked in the usual way. It wouldn't be the slightest challenge for the control freak in me. But Harriet and Luke? They were busy being college students. They were living life. They couldn't care less about stupid details.

Would that fact be fatal for me?

I wished now that my parents had a key to the house too. Wouldn't a mother have some sixth sense that something was amiss, even when everything was in its place? But my folks lived out in Connecticut — so they wouldn't just drop by without making a date. And unlike students, they didn't need a place in town where they could crash at short notice. We'd never even talked about them having a key. And now it was too late.

"And what about my employers?" I asked quietly, choosing to ignore his latest equivocal remark.

"That's been taken care of," he fired back. "They won't be expecting you for a while."

"So...you've written a resignation letter for me?"

My tone of voice surprised me. The words came out at least as hopefully as they did angrily.

"I'm not going to answer that. You don't need to know. There's only one thing you need to understand right now, and that's the fact that the sooner you cooperate, the better things will go for you.

"And if you're wondering, I mean *really* cooperating, Laura. No play-acting. I can tell the difference between genuine and fake, trust me. And I will do whatever is necessary to achieve true obedience from you. I have all the time in the world, but the longer you take to come round the more painful it's going to be."

I looked up at him, blinking fast. The choking was still fresh in my brain. I could feel a light layer of sweat forming on my temples.

"What does it mean...coming round?"

I *had* to understand what he wanted. Only then could I make some kind of plan to turn things my way.

"You will have come round when you obey every one of my commands without even a second of hesitation. You will have come round when your only thoughts will be of how you can please me. You will have come round when you accept that your body belongs to me and you *willingly* give it to me. You will have come round when I can be on the other side of the world and you are breathlessly waiting for my next order."

When he said that, I could only think of one thing.

"So...you're going to rape me?"

I held my breath as I waited for his answer. I looked away into the corner of the room, afraid to see the inevitable in his eyes.

"I don't *like* that word, Laura. Don't you dare ever use it again. It's something different from anything I do."

I suppressed a snort. Arrogant bastard. He thought he was above the law. Or that it wouldn't be rape if he forced himself on me, because I'd be so desperate to feel his power inside me.

Like I would ever want that now.

Chapter XIII

After Tommy left and my despair began to mount, so too did my hunger. My body was finally beginning to cry out for the essentials of life. The gnawing in my belly started to overpower the worry and fear around my imprisonment.

It overcame my embarrassment too. At some point on that Wednesday afternoon, it was like a switch flipped in me. My nudity just didn't seem important anymore. Where my fear of exposure had gotten me into this mess in the first place, now I felt like I'd have pressed my naked skin hard against the window if someone had flown by with a cheese sandwich. I guess starvation alters your priorities somewhat.

I had to get used to laying myself open anyway, because I simply couldn't keep still anymore. Only by changing position a lot was I able to maintain my sanity and take my mind off my body's most immediate need — sustenance.

So the relatively modest fetal position I'd generally kept fell by the wayside. Instead of sticking to the mat all the time, I spend periods standing against the wall, hands behind my back. As much as the chain around my ankle allowed, I paced back and forth. Sometimes I sat cross-legged. It all helped to keep my blood flowing, but I guess people could see whatever they wanted to see.

If he was filming me, well, fuck it. Maybe somebody on the internet would have enough of a brain to see I was being kept here against my will, rather than some cheap actress. I didn't know what to hope for anymore, other than food. How I would react on Tommy's next visit was anybody's guess, although I tried to train my brain not to be fooled into cheekiness when he turned up looking like a gentleman once more.

When would he come back, anyway? If he was going to rape me, why hadn't he just gotten it over with? Maybe I had misinterpreted his words yet again. If he wanted to rape someone, why not a beautiful young thing? And why rape *anybody* when you can get exactly the same result without risking jail? No, rape didn't make sense either.

Maybe the plan was simply to starve me into that 'obedience' thing that seemed to hold the key to wherever my life was going? If he deprived me of food for long enough, I supposed, then he would get whatever it was that he wanted. Maybe I would hold out for a while, but of course there would come a point where I would do anything to fill my belly. That would only be human, right?

But it didn't come to that. And when food came around dusk that evening, it didn't come from Tommy.

It was a woman.

I was standing against the wall when it happened. Hyper-sensitive to any hint of movement out there in the office space, I knew someone was out there even before the light snapped on in the open-plan area outside. I guessed the illumination worked on one of those motion-sensitive systems that jumped into life when somebody arrived on that floor of the building.

The light out there wasn't the kind of all-encompassing whiteness you'd expect from a fully-functioning office. It was more a soft yellow, like only a third of a bulbs were programmed to come on. So it took a while before my eyes fully focused on her approaching figure.

The woman had long, straight blonde hair, and wore a tight black dress with heels that pumped up her modest height just enough to give her a presence. It looked like she was on her way to a night at a cocktail bar, where she would flirt away with whatever guy might be bold enough to buy her a drink.

And there would be many volunteers, I was quite sure of that. She was knockout. But something about her way of moving irked me.

What was this woman doing here? I could somehow imagine Tommy sending his thug friends back over for a visit — but a good-looking girl like this? I hoped against hope that there was a great reason for it. That she'd somehow found out about the prisoner scandalously locked up in this building, and was coming to let me out.

As the blonde came closer, I noticed that her expression was almost unnaturally neutral. She looked me straight in the eyes, but I couldn't read anything from a distance. She didn't seem unhappy, but nor was she smiling. My heart sank a little as I saw how she moved, unhurried and carefree. Surely a would-be rescuer would be keen to get in and out as fast as possible?

I saw that she was carrying something in her hands. I watched her intently as she got up to the door and transferred the object to her right hand, touching the unlock mechanism with her left finger to gain access. She never once took her gaze off me. Her eyes were a captivating blue-green, with a hard-to-read intensity about them.

She stopped just inside the door. Neither of us said a word. Whose side was she on? Could I trust her? But she'd come here with such confidence, as though she had walked through that office many times before. And she'd let herself in the door like someone who knew my prison well. I guessed that made her no friend of mine.

Finally, her eyes left mine, but only to run slowly all the way down my figure. They slithered down my skin, stopped at my toes and then crawled back up my body once more. It was like she was sizing up a second-hand car and didn't want to give any of her impressions away to the dealer. She looked intently at every part, pausing extra-long on the bush just above my crotch. Suddenly I felt violated all over again, and covered my breasts with my forearm.

But then I noticed what the thing was that she carried, and I forgot to feel ashamed.

She had food. Nothing else mattered.

It was a large bowl. I couldn't see what was in it, but I could see the heat rising from it. And something smelled good. My stomach growled and started to do gymnastics.

"Who are you?" I asked.

I wanted the niceties — if that could possibly be the right word — to be over with as quickly as possible. I needed that hot food inside me. It was all I could do not to grab at that bowl.

"Oh, I'm Claire," she replied.

Her tone of voice was as even as her expression. Yet the note was husky, and dripped with a sensuality nobody could miss. Or maybe it was just the fact that her accent definitely wasn't from around here.

"Okay," I said, still on my guard. "And I don't suppose you're here to rescue me, are you?"

She gave me a quizzical look, as though I'd just asked her if she was able to speak English.

"No, of course not," she said blankly. "I'm just bringing you food. You must be hungry."

Of course I'm fucking hungry, you bitch-moron!

I kept the enraged screams in my head to myself and nodded as sweetly as I could. I needed her to bring that bowl of food over to me, and I would say (or not say) whatever it took to make that happen.

Her manner had every chance of rubbing me up the wrong way, but I didn't feel threatened. And that was a welcome feeling for my besieged soul. I was sure I could take her in a fair fight — but I was in chains.

Claire walked over towards me, legs criss-crossing like a model on a runway. She bent over at the waist, her dress tightening over her back like cling-wrap, and put the bowl on the floor at the foot of my mat.

She retreated a couple of steps towards the door, as if to make sure she wouldn't be within my reach if I made a sudden lunge at her.

There was no danger of that. I wasn't going to do anything that might jeopardize this meal. I might even have turned down a wide-open door at that moment.

"Spaghetti," she said. "*Bon appétit.*"

Aha, that was it! She'd wished me a good meal in what sounded like a perfect accent for that particular phrase. Claire had to be French. Or Swiss. Or Belgian.

But the nuances of her nationality didn't hold my attention for more than a second. Only one thing could do that right now.

I looked at her and then at the bowl on the floor. Clearly the food was not going to come any closer to me. I was going to have to go over and get it.

This was no time to follow polite dining protocols. I stepped out and grabbed the bowl before she had time to change her mind and take it away. She might have wished me a good feed in a sexy accent, but I wasn't in the most trusting of moods.

I sat down on my mat, holding the warm bowl between my hands. The heat of the spaghetti, which was covered in a meaty-looking sauce, hit me in the face. My mouth began to water and the last, lingering discomfort from Tommy's attack on my throat melted away as the thought of soft pasta and sauce sliding down it overcame me.

I may have been a prisoner in the most desperate and demeaning captivity, but in that moment I was elated. Food! I had food!

What I didn't have, I quickly realized as I looked to take my first bite, was anything to eat it with. No knife, fork or spoon. Just me and my bowl.

I glanced up at Claire. I didn't have the energy for this! My mouth was gushing saliva as I embarked on this stupid conversation that was getting in the way of my feast.

"How do I eat it?"

She raised an eyebrow. I spelled it out.

"I mean, I have no knife or fork."

"You just eat it. You have your mouth. Don't use your hands, they get dirty. I recommend it's easier if you keep it on the floor."

Now it was my turn to raise an eyebrow. *Recommend* was a strange choice of word. It was like she spoke from experience.

"You mean eat like a dog?"

"It's your choice," she shrugged. "You can do it as you want, I just tell you what I think is best."

I wanted to quiz her so badly. I knew I could learn something from this Claire, whoever she was. But right now hunger was the only desire I could heed. My stomach was screaming at me to get my priorities straight.

I nodded at her, trying not to look frustrated by this unnecessary madness regarding the cutlery situation. I was just hoping she would take the hint to leave and let me demean myself without a live audience. God knows who might have been watching through the cameras or the screen, but at least I could put remote eyes to the back of my mind more easily.

Claire nodded back, betraying no emotion in particular, and turned towards to the door.

The entrance to my cell had barely clicked back into the lock position before I brought the bowl up towards my mouth. I stayed sitting on my mat. I was determined to do this in a vaguely dignified way if I could get away with it.

In the event, I don't think I would have managed to be dignified even with a full set of cutlery and a seat at a neatly-laid table. The nearer the food got to my mouth, the harder the extent of my famishment kicked in. I did not stand on ceremony as I grabbed that first mouthful.

And then I really got going. I forgot all about watching Claire's exit. I just lost myself in that food. I slurped and lapped my way through the spaghetti, tipping the bowl this way and that as I wrapped my lips around anything I could get a grip on. And I sure as hell didn't care how I looked. My situation was too ridiculous for that anyway.

The meal was rich, tasty and filling. When I had finally licked out the last of the bowl and put it down on the carpet, I went blank with a deep, beautiful satisfaction. For a short while I forgot my troubles. It was without doubt the finest moment of my forced stay in this place. Pretty much the only fine moment, in fact.

No doubt my nose was covered in sauce and my mouth was stained. I could feel stickiness coating half of my face. But I hadn't eaten with the bowl on the floor, doggy-style. And that felt like a small victory of sorts.

I could feel an intense new life force rushing into my body. Buoyed by sustenance, my heart beat quick and my blood ran fast. My body temperature was up, and a dusting of perspiration pricked at the roots of my hair. I was almost hyperventilating, too, and it felt like it would take several minutes for my breathing to come back to normal. It was a little like I'd just had sex.

I sat there with my head hanging and my hair straggling across my face, dazed with pleasure. There was nowhere to go and I was in no hurry to drop down from the high. I felt pretty sure this mood wasn't going to last very long, so I just let myself ride the wave.

With the nourishment I'd suddenly been allowed, everything seemed possible. I was strong again. I would find a way to outsmart Tommy. I would fight my way out of here. It was ridiculous to allow myself to be locked up like this, so deep into the twenty-first century. Things couldn't possibly be as bad as they had seemed. It was all going to work out just fine.

I began to feel my senses return to me. I felt my chest slow its heaving. My vision came back into focus, and I looked around the room with renewed optimism and interest.

The lights in the main office had gone off. I hoped that meant Claire had disappeared.

I tried not to think about her lurking behind one of those abandoned desks like a statue, watching me so quietly that the lighting system had timed itself out. With such an expanse of dark, open space out there, dotted as it was with extra-black blobs of furniture, it was easy to imagine scary things. Things that moved.

Less frightening, but way more creepy, was the thought that someone could be watching me via video. But I cared far less about that camera with a full stomach. I wiped my mouth and my face with the back of my right hand, and then with my left. That felt better!

With the feeding frenzy over and the capacity to think about other things returning, I puzzled over Claire. I'd gotten used to a single foe. Tommy, Tommy, Tommy. The two guys who'd caught me notwithstanding, I'd assumed Tommy was at the centre of everything. I hadn't had a single thought of escape that didn't involve tricking Tommy, outwitting Tommy or giving Tommy the slip.

Now I seemed to be dealing with more people. And unlike the henchmen who had brought me here two nights earlier, I couldn't place how Claire fitted into the picture. Was she just a glorified servant whom Tommy paid to run errands like bringing me food? That was a crazy notion — a random worker would go to the police straight away when they saw what was going on up here.

The sultry French girl hadn't seemed remotely surprised to see me naked and chained. Nor even sympathetic. Sure, you could brief somebody about what they might expect to see on an assignment. You might even tell them that everything is legal; that the woman they're bringing food to is a sexual deviant who has begged to be kept in prison — that was a thing, wasn't it? — but even then there'd be a curiosity in their manner. Wouldn't there?

Something made me feel sure that Claire had been to this place before. Either that, or she'd seen everything she needed to see via video. I imagined her sitting in some sinister monitoring room right now, watching me. In my head she was next to Tommy, their shoulders touching as they eyeballed the captive.

Weird, too, that she had given me advice about how to eat. Was that just what Tommy had told her to say? Or had she seen this challenge before? *Maybe you're not the first one in here.*

I looked across at the built-in toilet. It seemed crazy to think that such a prison amenity would be built just for me. This whole thing seemed a big investment for...whatever it was he was planning with me. He must have rented or bought the building, or at least this entire floor. How else could he ensure nobody else came up here?

And yet, I'd only met Tommy two days ago! Sure, I had the feeling he had known about *me* a little longer than that, but this kind of setup must take a bit of effort no matter how good your connections are. The kind of effort you'd go to just for one troublesome woman at Kerstein?

The more I thought about it, the more I wondered if Tommy did this *thing* on a routine basis. My heart pounded at the thought. If others had been here, then where were they now? Was Claire one of them?

I tried to steer my thoughts away from the awful possibilities. Instead, I focussed on the latest affirmation that killing me wasn't on the cards. Namely, the fact that I'd been given food. Food that was, from his point of view, unnecessarily good. If he'd wanted me dead, after all, he could have just let me starve quietly.

Also, if Claire *was* some sort of graduate of this room, then she was patently alive. That would be another reason to believe Tommy wasn't in the murder game. But then she was French and sexy! So did he like to capture beautiful women or business counterparts? I couldn't work it out. Or maybe he only let the beautiful business counterparts live...

This thinking was wearing me out. I had ten times as many questions as answers, and I was too full of food to tax my brain for very long. Claire's appearance meant I'd at least picked up one piece of the puzzle tonight. I wasn't at all sure where it was going to fit in, but it was a fragment of knowledge to cherish.

Right now, I felt ready to wash myself. I could feel the crustiness of dried food around my mouth already.

I groaned as I hoisted myself up onto my feet, feeling like a deadweight. Still hampered by my chain, I shuffled over to the sink and washed my hands as best I could. There was no soap.

I splashed water on the bottom half of my face, and rubbed hard with my fingers. Soon my lips and the surrounding skin felt normal again. But without a mirror I couldn't know if I'd removed all the stains.

I wasn't sure I really wanted to see my reflection right now, anyway. If I looked anywhere as messy as I felt, the sight would only drag me down. There was definitely no way I could match up to Claire, that was for sure.

I shrugged as I took a long drink of water from the tap.

Then I straightened up, feeling light-headed for a moment. I guessed my body was struggling to process a meal after two days without a morsel. It had been a heavy feed, too. In some ways it was an even bigger shock to the system than getting kidnapped.

But I was going to handle it. Digesting a meal was the least of the troubles I had to worry about right now, and for who knew how many days or weeks to come. I steadied myself against the edge of the sink, and the woozy moment passed.

Then, without warning, a long, deep yawn seized me. My eyelids thickened, all of a sudden threatening to close on me if I didn't take them to bed right now.

If I'd slept at all since I'd been here, it hadn't been for more than a couple of minutes at a time. The kind of stolen nap you're not even sure happened at all. Now, finally filled with food and feeling warm, I felt overcome with fatigue.

I was happy about that. I had wanted to be exhausted. That was the only way I'd be able to pass out when my mind was strangled with fear, embarrassment and worry. Scrutinizing everything in this room all day long wasn't going to help. I wanted nothing more than to blank my mind and be left alone for a few hours. And now, at last, my body was crying out for real rest.

Right now I no longer cared who that Claire woman was, what Tommy's plans were or even about the fact that he had all of my clothes. Escape could wait for tomorrow. Yawning non-stop, I crossed back to my mat and curled up on my side.

It was as uncomfortable as ever, but I could have slept on the cold stone floor of a cave just then. My eyes were so heavy that I had no say in whether they closed or not. They just did.

I drifted off into real sleep. It wasn't sweet and it wasn't deep, but it was definitely sleep.

And in that moment, bad sleep was the only escape I could hope for.

Chapter XIV

My slumber was better than I could ever have hoped. I must have woken up every twenty minutes that night, but under the circumstances it was a good rest. The mattress wasn't terrible to lie on, but there still wasn't much softness between me on the floor. If I stayed in any position for too long my bones would start to hurt. And I didn't even have a blanket. So any sleep was great sleep.

Even when dawn began to filter into the room, and I woke up for what felt like the ninety-fifth time, I rolled over and passed out once more. Twenty more minutes. Twenty more minutes. It kept happening. I began to wonder if my eyes would ever stay open for good.

Not that I particularly wanted to wake up. *Grab the sleep while you can. It's not like you have anything to get up for. Another choking, maybe?*

It was bright outside by the time I'd finally had enough of sleeping. My eyelids were still reluctant to open wide enough for me to see past my lashes, but I could feel my brain waking up. This time I sensed I wasn't going to collapse again.

I stretched my body. Every muscle and bone ached. My calf tried to cramp. *Take it real slow now, Laura.*

My throat seemed to have recovered from yesterday, at least. But there was an unpleasant feeling deep in my stomach. I knew it well from my life outside this cell. The same gut-twisting worry that woke me every time I had a difficult meeting looming. Every time I knew a tricky email lay in wait. I didn't want that feeling now. I didn't need it in here.

Couldn't last night's wonderful after-dinner feeling come back instead? I longed to be able to reach into my own fridge. To be able to get that sated stomach back anytime I wanted. What had I *done* to deserve this purgatory?

My eyes were crusty with sleep. I dug into their corners with my thumb and forefinger, gouging out the sandiness. I wouldn't be fully awake until cold water met the skin on my face, but at least I was starting to take things in as I rolled off my throbbing right shoulder and sat upright.

I blinked as I looked towards the window. The blue-sky weather was gone, but the clouds were high. Well, it made a change.

Only then did I notice Tommy.

He was standing on the other side of the see-through door, watching me, impassive as a statue. My heart skipped a beat and my stomach coiled even tighter as I registered his ominous presence. All thoughts of sleep vanished like magic.

How long had he been hovering there? I stared at him, a scowl spreading across my face. He'd gone casual today — clearly he wasn't on his way to a meeting at my office. A navy blue polo shirt that exposed a solid neck and a sculpted throat. Loose-fitting denim pants, his hands thrust in the pockets. The buckle of his black leather belt gleamed like it had been polished that very morning. I wanted to ignore the fact that he was attractive as well as ominous, but I couldn't quite manage it. He stared right back at me.

I sighed. Where was this going? How much of that spirit that I'd gone to sleep with remained with me now? You think you know how you're going to react to things — but you never really know until the moment comes.

Tommy's jawline was set even firmer than I could remember seeing before, as if he was clenching his teeth or chewing gum. Suddenly I remembered that I was probably supposed to kneel. But before I could give that any thought, he jerked his head to his right. That drew my gaze towards the screen in front of me.

For the first time since I'd been brought here, the device was displaying words. White letters on a jet-black background.

Open your legs. Touch yourself.

The only surprising thing about the message was that it didn't surprise me. I hadn't wanted to admit it to myself until now, but I guess something inside me must have known it would eventually come to this. That it would get overtly and unequivocally sexual. I guess I didn't want to reconcile something that should have been so sweet with this bitter experience.

But with this latest command, there was no more fooling myself that this had nothing to do with my being a woman. That he just wanted to terrorize me, humiliate me and imprison me for some business goal I didn't understand. He had, after all, declined ample opportunity to rape me, and I'd begun to feel sure it had to be something else.

Now, with this latest twist playing out on the screen in front of me, I had to see it in a new light. If I looked past all the weirdness, Tommy really did want me for sexual ends.

Three mornings ago, my heart would have leapt to know that. Now, under these circumstances, the idea did not fill me with pleasure.

After all, he was going to continue treating me like dirt. It looked like he would get to those sexual ends in a drawn-out, convoluted way. I guess a straightforward rape wouldn't have satisfied whatever fetishes possessed him. This whole thing was a twisted game to my captor. Why *wouldn't* he give me his sick, perverted instructions by putting them on a screen? Of *course* he would want to watch my still-sleepy face screw up in horror as I took in the words.

Well, I wasn't going to give him that satisfaction. If he wanted to toy with his prey, torturing it instead of overpowering it like he knew he could, then his prey wasn't going to be a very accommodating plaything.

Knowing that I was about to be defiant once again, my body shot adrenaline through my system as I forced my head to turn in his direction. I fought to keep my face expressionless, like a robot that simply wasn't going to process the request made of it.

I looked into his eyes. My legs stayed closed. My hands remained still, palms flat on the floor and fingers splayed wide.

Tommy raised one eyebrow.

I looked away to the window. I really didn't want to see what might be coming.

At any moment I was sure the door would open and my captor would fly into the room in a rage. But I didn't hear so much as a twitch. And when I dared to look back across to that far right-hand corner, Tommy had a phone in his hand. He was typing something.

At least it wasn't *my* phone this time. This one was larger and bulkier, halfway to being a tablet.

As he typed, movement on the screen in front of me caught my eye. New letters were appearing one by one —

and I suspected they were the same ones he was putting into the keyboard he held.

Repeat...open...your...legs....wide...

There was no doubt he was writing in real time. What a game to play. My eyes narrowed as I waiting for the rest of the message to display, one word at a time.

...and...slide...two...fingers...deep...inside...
your...pussy...

Was that a twinge of anticipation I just felt?

How...fuck, now that was a *real* surprise. Was it seeing the words 'inside your pussy' and the mental image that came with it? My eyes opened wide and I hitched my breath. But my right hand rested just where it was.

I dared not read the message a second time. I looked at Tommy again. He met my gaze with a hint of mocking in his eyes. My resolve steeled once again. This brute would *not* watch me fold like a helpless fairy.

With the tiniest movement, so small at first that I didn't know exactly when it had stopped being a thought and started being an action, I shook my head. Clenching my teeth, I summoned up the strength to do it clearly. Or at least firmly enough to be understood. Once to the right. Then to the left. Another to the right. Then I stopped. Looked straight ahead.

I stared blankly at the glass beneath the screen, studiously and conspicuously avoiding the words upon it. I waited. Legs closed. Hands unmoved.

Sure, I wanted to look calm in my contempt for his blunt demands. But I wasn't breathing at all. *He's going to snap any second.*

What had I got myself into now? Part of me didn't want to know and wouldn't let me look across at him again. I could see he was still there, standing on the other side of the door. But the corner of my eye wouldn't tell me anything more. Was he wearing a look of thunder already?

Tick-tick-tick.

What was that?

The sound was coming from the monitor in front of me. Instinctively I looked up at it. The instruction had been wiped.

Tick-tick-tick.

Exactly the same sound an old-fashioned standing clock would make. I'd never considered that this wall-mounted screen could produce audio as well as images and light. The thought that it could start doing that in the middle of the night filled me with dread.

Then something on the monitor caught my eye. I was into some kind of countdown. Synchronised perfectly to the ticking sound, numbers appeared in the middle of the top half of the screen. The same uncompromising white font. Sixty. Fifty-nine. Fifty-eight.

I had less a minute. *Until what?*

Fifty-seven. Fifty-six.

I deliberately looked away. Not at him, but not at the screen either. I contemplated the ceiling, feeling a light, anxious perspiration break out on my forehead.

Tick-tick-tick.

Fifty-three. Fifty-two. Fifty-one.

As I brought my eyes back down to focus sullenly on some distant point with no significance whatsoever, I noticed that words had joined the numbers on the display. This time the letters were red.

I had to read it. Your heart can be filled with dread, but still you crave to know what that message for you says.

This...is...your...final...chance...

The letters were appearing one by one again. And Tommy wasn't done yet.

*...Recommend...you...do...as...you...have...
been...instructed...or...your...grace...period...
ends...here...*

I stared at the ever-swelling text the way a tired dog stares at an over-energetic, ball-throwing child on a scorching day. I watched as the numbers ticked below thirty. And I was the last person on earth who could tell you what I was going to do. My reactions now were reduced to primal drives. Preservation. Protection. Honour. Pride. But in which order?

I thought about the pain Tommy had already inflicted on me. It seemed more than reasonable to assume something dire would occur if I didn't comply in the next few seconds.

This was about pride versus pain. Only how could I talk about pride when I was being kept like this? Pride had long since disappeared. That was the fact of the matter, and it was stupid to pretend otherwise. Avoiding pain, on the other hand, seemed to be something I could control. Maybe it was logical to obey.

Ten. Nine. Eight. Seven.

Keeping my eyes set dead-straight ahead of me, I forced my right hand down between my legs. I opened them just enough. Grinding my teeth, I paired my index and middle fingers. Clenching my jaw, I sent them towards my long-neglected entrance. Setting my face like stone, I pushed them inside my slit.

Two. One. Just in time.

But my God, this felt good.

While I stared straight on, I swear I could see Tommy wolf-grinning in the corner.

And suddenly I knew just what that feeling in my stomach had been. It wasn't worry I'd woken up with. It was pure arousal.

A tiny murmur of pleasure slipped out of my mouth. It had escaped before I could stop it. Fuck, what if he heard that? And worse, what if my face was showing some of the distraction I was feeling?

I closed my eyes, hoping to dull some of my senses. But it only made that longing to move my fingers all the more present. They weren't in very far past my entrance — that had been my protest. Now, my thumb itched to brush over my clitoris. I was in a holding pattern that might very well not be sustainable.

The idea that I was being filmed for some obscene broadcast made its way back into my mind. Only this time, with my legs tingling to spread wider and my pussy begging me to push past the second knuckle, I didn't find the notion so disagreeable at all. I was captive, after all, wasn't I? It wouldn't be my fault. Nothing that happened here could be my fault.

Then I heard the door opening. My head turned sideways towards Tommy, who stood on the threshold and watched me without a word. I fervently hoped my face didn't look the way it felt in that moment: wide-eyed, inviting, drunken.

I shivered suddenly. Partly fear, partly a slight chill in the room. But a little bit of something else, too. My body was on high alert.

"Smart girl," said Tommy. The words oozed out like a slow trail of syrup. He rolled each 'r' as though he had all day to get to the next letter. The way he said 'girl', turning it into a two-syllable word that sounded like a stream tripping over pebbles, had me quivering. Was there any manlier way on earth to say that word?

I didn't reply to him. My brain was a tangled mess. For the first time since being brought here, I was feeling those things I'd felt the first time he walked into our conference room. Why now?

"Seems like you respond well to being prompted in writing," he said, closing the door and slowly making his way towards me. "It must be the lawyer in you. Interesting."

Still I didn't reply. What could I say to any of this?

I wanted to forget that I was a chained-up, beaten-down captive. Could Tommy, of all people, be the one to take my mind off things for a moment?

He seemed unperturbed by my non-answers as he strolled over to stand in front of the screen, which was now blank. He wasn't in the slightest hurry today. It was almost as though he was in a good mood. And now here he was, staring down at my naked, self-penetrating body, with something like approval.

My position was as modest as it could be under the circumstances. I felt a sudden urge to draw my feet towards my hips, bringing my knees up and parting my legs further. I battled it with every fibre of my being. I could *not* show what I was feeling.

"It's good to see you showing a little — how do you law people like to put it? — *compliance*." He chuckled at his own joke. Where was he going with this? Was I finally about to find out, after all, that this kidnapping had everything to do with business?

"Yes, well, compliance is easier to get when you threaten people with violence," I said. Something in the vibe made me feel a little braver today. But had I said it a touch too bitterly?

I could think of more than one reason not to piss Tommy off right now.

To my surprise, he smiled.

"Yes, I've found that to be the case," he grinned. "You're beginning to understand, Laura. But you know, I much prefer it when a woman doesn't need to be coerced. Or bribed." He put his hands on his knees, bending down low enough for me to hear what he whispered next. "It's much sexier that way…"

The accent again. That 'r'. Jesus, was there any sexier way for a man to say 'sexier'?

I felt my nose twitch, like a deer sniffing the autumn air. A doe who's just found a scent, maybe.

"Now you understand where I'm coming from," he announced, straightening up again, "let me level with you. A question, first. Would you like to be released?"

Well, duh.

But what came out of my mouth was this: "What, right now?"

Fuck, had I lost my mind?

Tommy's smile changed. He could read me like a dirty book. A look of satisfaction flooded his features.

"No, not right now," he smirked. "Nor any time soon. I mean at some point in the future."

"Yes, obviously," I tried to snap. It was so overplayed that he ignored my tone of voice completely.

"Well, Laura, then *compliance* will be your ticket," he continued. "If you're well-behaved and do as you're told, with a smile and enthusiasm, and when *none* of it is faked, then your chances are good. You might even be able to go back to that office you love so much."

He jerked his head in the direction of Kerstein's building. Clearly Tommy was well aware of this perch's ironic positioning. His expression, however, suggested he had doubts about just how much I really wanted to get back to that desk of mine.

"If I have to constantly *threaten* you," he continued. "I might run out of patience…"

He walked deliberately over to the window. I watched him put his hands in his pockets and gaze out over New York City. The rational side of me wanted to quiz him. What, exactly, would happen if he ran out of patience? And how far did *compliance* actually extend? These were big questions.

But instead, as I found my fingers worming their way a little deeper inside me, I found myself entirely consumed by the way the material of his pants had tightened over his ass.

"So you see, Laura, it's entirely in your own hands."

His voice reverberated strangely off the glass.

His butt looked made of steel. The buildings of the city formed the perfect backdrop. I think I might have been holding my breath. I know that my fingers curled ever-deeper inside of me, feeling out that magic spot. And somewhere down at the bottom of my body, my toes curled too.

Tommy turned around and looked at me, one eyebrow raised. He wanted an answer.

"I understand," I murmured. I hoped that was enough to satisfy him for the moment. I couldn't mull over a strategy in my current state. And until that had happened, I couldn't start agreeing to *compliance* — or otherwise.

"Excellent," he said, seemingly happy with my answer. And the way he had understood it became abundantly clear a moment later as he strode back towards my mat on the floor and began to unzip his trousers.

Chapter XV

I could feel my pussy gush from the moment I saw what was happening. My heart began to thud. It was useless to pretend that my body wasn't getting just the thing it craved right now.

There was nothing for it but to submit to my base instincts. I'd had enough of living like this, consumed by thoughts about the unfairness of it all. Enough self-loathing and enough Tommy-loathing. I needed a little holiday from the effort of despising one of such raw beauty.

Take me, Tommy. I couldn't say it out loud. But the words howled around my head like a Midwestern tornado.

"Stand up," he ordered. "And keep those fingers in your pussy."

A new seriousness had crept into his tone. His breathing was deeper and his throat tighter. He unbuckled his pants, not taking his eyes off me for a second.

Then he grabbed me by the throat. But only hard enough to show me who was boss. Both hands wrapped around it, ready to steer me. To push me where he wanted me to go. With one hand buried between my legs and a chain around my ankle I would struggle for balance, but I found the fingers of my left hand clutching his loosened belt as he stepped in close, nudging me backwards towards the wall.

The back of my head hit the paintwork with a slightly painful thud, but I barely noticed the discomfort. I was transfixed, stunned, waiting for the next thing he would do to me.

"Pull down my pants," he growled. "And sink into a squat as you go."

I moved to obey him, then stopped myself. Was I really supposed to do this with one hand?

"Should I still...keep my right hand where it is?" I asked him. Where in the world had that sweet, willing tone of voice come from?

"Yes. Never undo a command unless you're told to do so."

I nodded, and began to work my way around the top of his pants with my one free hand. I pulled one part down an inch or so, then moved on around the waist. It was clumsy going, but still I remembered to gradually bend my knees and begin to squat down as more and more of his black, taut boxers began to appear.

"Actually, I want you to make a slight adjustment. Take your fingers out and put your thumb inside instead. Curl it down, towards the floor."

I was halfway into my squat, legs spread and bent like an Indian dancer frozen into sculpted stone. I did as he asked. My thumb felt cool and small in comparison to the two thoroughly-soaked fingers.

"Your third finger will be sopping wet. I want you to slide it into your asshole. Clear?"

My heart raced harder. My eyes opened wide in surprise. I hesitated. Nothing had ever been in there. I'd always shied away from that idea. Too painful, too strange, I'd always thought. Things were getting extreme already.

But the slight pause wasn't enough to make Tommy react. I moved to do as he said before he could question my resolve. It seemed I would follow his every command this morning. I didn't know what this force was that was pushing me to obedience. But I wanted to keep on letting it guide me. Where would we go together?

With no further instructions and no experience to speak of, I simply went for it. Anchoring my hand firmly with my thumb inside my pussy, I located my anus with my third finger. Sensing Tommy's impatience, I pushed my finger at the tight hole, pad first, and hoped that would work.

At first I felt a resistance, but after a moment or two of pressure, my hole seemed to suck my finger inside with a gulp. An odd sensation of fullness rippled up from between my legs. My finger had become larger than life. And the combination was making my creaking knees tremble.

"I've done that," I said, with just a little croak in my voice. And then something made me want to add, "my fingers are in."

"Keep up that compliance," said Tommy heavily. "And continue taking down my pants."

I carried on taking down his trousers one-handed. After a couple of minutes I had them at his ankles. I'd felt the firm flesh of his legs against my fingers and thumb as I'd helped the fabric down over his thighs, knees and calves. He had a light scattering of hair in all of the right places, and a small, blue-green tattoo I didn't recognize on the outside of his lower left-leg. I already longed to revisit this. To breathe in the scent of light sweat and body spray. To taste the skin.

I had all my weight on my haunches, my legs wide open as I double-penetrated myself. Having sunk lower down, it was easier to hold my froggy position. My mind flitted for just a moment to the wide open spaces of the outer office. What if someone else came snooping? *Now is not the moment to start caring about that, Laura!*

Now I was face to face with a sizeable something straining at Tommy's underwear. I felt a bizarre pride that I had a part to play in that bulge. I looked up at him, ready to hear his next order. I wanted it to involve more undressing.

"Take it out and lick the tip," he said, the words now fizzing out through gritted teeth. "You'll find a drop or two there. Get them on your tongue and swallow them."

A high-school dance energy pulsed through my thighs when he spoke these words. The thrill was almost too much. I pinched my buried thumb and finger closer together within my body as I let his order sink in. I could feel each digit with the other, through the thin separation between the inside of my ass and the inside of my vagina.

How had things turned so quickly? How did I let this happen?

Steadying my squat, I placed my left hand on the front of his boxers. I wrapped my fingertips around the elastic clamping the top of the garment to his skin. Then I eased it towards me and down. He'd asked me to take it out, not to take them off, so I stuck to the letter of the law and made a grab for his shaft as soon as I had enough of his shorts out of the way.

Spurred on by the penetration down below, I was almost convulsing with lust as I took his thick, meaty cock in my hand. My body and my mind had switched to total surrender. It was not a feeling with which I had much experience, but it was making me horny as fuck. Tommy's plump, healthy manhood filled my palm. Soft to the touch, yet rigid at the core, it begged to be toyed with. I was about to succumb to instinct and slide the skin along his length, when I remember the exact order he'd given me. I had to follow his playbook to the word.

I switched my focus from the pulsing flesh in my hand to the pink dome before my eyes. It was just like he had said: a globule of translucence glistened at the apex. It was loaded with promise. Bottom-heavy as it crept further out of its lair, it looked on the verge of letting go. I had no doubt that another was waiting in the wings.

Before that droplet could get away, I found myself wriggling forward and moistening my tongue. And the feeling, as my mouth and his cock drew closer to each other, was one of honour. I was *proud* to be the one chosen for this task right now. What had come over me? How had I been tricked? Or had I really been in denial throughout these days?

I landed my tongue directly on the little white beacon. A microdose of saltiness, wetness and potency. I tried to let the tiny treat slip down my throat, but my saliva engulfed it long before it got there. Now the next drop awaited my attentions; I dealt with that too. Again it melted away. Tommy certainly knew how to make you ache for more.

My knees were beginning to hurt from the squat, and my twisted hand was starting to feel a little uncomfortable, but those very discomforts were a thrill I didn't want to give up. Tommy had put me where I was. And maybe I was out of my mind — but I relished his next instruction.

But it wasn't an instruction that came next. Just action. The moment I looked inquiringly up towards him, his shaft still in my loose grip, was the moment he jerked his hips back, pulling it out of my hand before I knew what was happening. He took two steps back, but didn't say a word.

He surveyed me with a determined look, a slight twitch twisting the left corner of his mouth in a way I'd not noticed before. Never taking his gaze off me, he bent down, loosened each of his shoelaces, then kicked off each of his shoes. He stepped out of his trousers.

Naked from the waist down, he looked no less mouthwatering. His muscular legs, dark and tanned in perfect accord with his face and hands, looked strong enough to hold up a house. His socks were a rich navy blue and I was able to appreciate the true enormity of his feet. He had to be a size 14.

And then he came at me. Fast. Instinctively, I backed up harder against the wall, bracing myself as my pulse quickened to what felt like breaking point.

Still without a sound beyond his heavy, assured intakes of breath, he gripped my lower jaw with his forefingers. Hard. Without ceremony he pushed his thumb at my lips, taking my own breath away. As soon as I understood he wanted in, I let my mouth fall open. And in he came.

He lay his thumb right across the width of my mouth, pressing its pad hard on my back-right teeth. So anchored, he fixed his opposing fingers firm around my chin. It wasn't uncomfortable, but still it felt like every ounce of power in his body had been channeled into this vice-hold around my jaw. My tongue had nowhere else to go but to rest on his thumbnail. I tried to resist letting it explore this new sensation, looking for another injection of saltiness. But I couldn't stop the saliva gathering fast underneath my curious, hungry tongue.

I thought I was close to the wall. But when Tommy took me by this strong, intriguing new grip and shoved my body against it, I realized just how much harder my back still could be pressed onto the paintwork. Forced to adjust my knees and my ankles once more, and still to keep my thumb and finger in their respective openings at my core, I let out a gasp. My loudest yet.

The intensity in the room was rising by the second. I could sense that the time for slow and gentle was over.

Now my back was taking some of the weight off my knees. I could balance them against the unyielding wall just a little. It brought my body position higher than before.

And that came in handy when Tommy yanked his hand away from my drooling mouth, plunged his cock deep inside it and began to throat-fuck me.

Chapter XVI

I was covered in sweat and gasping like a woman just rescued from drowning. I could do nothing but clutch at the oxygen around me as I lay in a naked, wheezing heap on the floor. Tommy had just left the room. The taste of his cock was still strong in my mouth.

Tommy had rammed his manhood down my throat for several minutes, forcing it to open up and take him repeatedly. It had made the experience with my own fingers seem like a mere warm-up. I'd thought then that he'd taken me close to my limits, but this morning's onslaught had shown me how much more I could endure. Surely, though, *this* battering was on the edge for me.

Somehow I didn't gag. I had always assumed that I would do so if somebody tried something like that — though George never did — and I had certainly never gone looking for opportunities to deep-throat. But now it seemed like I could handle an assault on that part of my body without throwing up. That was a positive thing, of course — but why did I feel a hint of pride about it? I wanted to be a hundred percent outraged at Tommy's sexual assault, the latest in a growing line of offences. And yet here I was, a part of me silently revelling in my throat's performance as I lay crumpled on the floor. What was that about?

And why wasn't I utterly incensed about the sticky streaks of semen across my torso? Tommy had chosen not to come in my mouth — would I have been mad if he did? — but instead pulled out at the critical moment and released his hot seed all over my collarbone. As I squatted there against the wall, it had immediately begun to course its way around and between my breasts.

He'd put his cock straight back in after that, forcing me to suck it clean as his erection died down ever so slowly. I hadn't done that kind of thing since before the kids were born — and to be honest I had never missed that salty, sickly taste. Today, though, I'd accepted with a certain relish. What was happening to me?

I guessed the rage would come back quickly enough. I'd been horny as fuck and to my shame I had succumbed to that. I had still been horny as fuck when Tommy had withdrawn for the last time, rearranged his pants and left the room. I was *still* horny as fuck right now. This was real torture.

It took a good few minutes to regain normal breathing and return to my senses. Sure enough, the pissed-off side of me was beginning to win out already. I wanted to bring myself to release and I was mad that my only option was to do so in what I had to assume was full public view. I didn't want to show him that he'd left me full of lust and dying to come, even though my desire could hardly have escaped him. Seeing my desperation now would be exactly what he wanted — fuck that!

I needed to use the toilet, and that made me mad too. Nothing could restore my fury quite like having to relieve myself in that undignified, legs-open perch that my chains forced me to adopt. And in front of at least one camera. Not even Andre could be as mean as this!

Not that I wanted to see Andre right now. Escape, yes. I wanted to get out. But that office? I felt sure that I would slap Andre right across the face the moment I got there. I had an odd certainty about it. It was as if this whole ordeal had awakened some kind of fighting confidence in me. At least when it came to my unloved colleague.

A short while later, Claire appeared in the doorway. She was carrying a tray. Breakfast time! I cheered up immediately.

Today the blonde was wearing a wispy white blouse with blue jeans and white sneakers. The blouse, which bordered on being see-through, left her shoulders bare. Even from a distance you could see how tanned and smooth they were. Her hair was tied in a ponytail. How could she be so naturally sexy in two completely different outfits? And why did she get to wear clothes while I didn't? It just wasn't fair.

"You are hungry, I guess? I hope you like scrambled eggs?"

I love scrambled eggs, but I tried not to jump for joy. Why should I show gratitude to this glorified jailer? I just nodded.

But I sensed a friendlier vibe from her as she came over to me. It was as though she didn't think I was going to bite her or scratch her this time around. She even bore a trace of a smile, or at least a glint in her eye. Why? My mind raced. Did we share some kind of bond now that Tommy had done *that* to me? A bond like that didn't make me want to smile. The mere thought brought a jealous scowl across my face.

"*Bon appétit,*" she said once more.

"Thanks," I said, trying not to be bitchy. I didn't know her circumstances at all. Maybe she too was a captive. And whatever she was, it wouldn't hurt to get on her good side.

"I'll be back in 30 minutes," she said as she left the room. "We have some grooming to do."

She closed the door before I had a chance to press her on exactly what that might mean. I shrugged to myself. Whatever it was, there was nothing I could do to influence it, so I might as well enjoy eating. On the tray sat a round, white plate with two slices of toast and a dollop of scrambled eggs on top of each. Again there was no cutlery, but this was meal you would eat with your hands anyway. A tall glass of orange juice completed the picture.

The juice burned my exhausted throat a little as it went down, but it tasted amazing. It was properly fresh-squeezed, direct from the fruit. The toast was crispy to perfection and the eggs were creamy with a touch of saltiness. It was an odd touch that the food was so fine in this cell of mine. The cuisine was the only thing here that gave me any sense of worth. It flew in the face of everything else that was happening to me, right down to the absence of a knife and fork.

I had a sudden longing for a coffee. Was it wrong to be thinking about a *latte* in such a grave situation? I wasn't sure, but I could see a good argument for living the best life I could under the circumstances.

I tried not to gobble too much and focus on savouring the food. Such pleasures looked like they would be rare. And it wasn't like I had anywhere to be. Apart from the 'grooming' appointment I was choosing not to think about.

Breakfast was sitting comfortably in my stomach by the time Claire returned to the room. This time she was carrying a small bucket and a brown leather pouch that fit snugly into her hand. I could see steam rising from the bucket. Over her shoulder she carried a small pink towel. *Oh God.*

In an instant I switched from the relative contentedness that came with a meal to nervous worry. What was she going to do to me? I couldn't help imagining the worst. Some form of mutilation couldn't be out of the question if Tommy was behind this. Which I assumed he was.

I watched her put everything down on the floor just out of my reach. "Don't worry," she said with a half-smile as she left the room again — she didn't actually bother to shut the door this time — and disappeared around the corner in the direction of the elevators. A few seconds later she emerged once more, this time carrying a wide, stumpy wooden stool. She closed the door of my cell behind her and put the stool against the back wall, halfway between my mattress and the window. She placed the towel over the stool.

"Please sit on the stool," she said in her patient, even tone.

My eyes narrowed. It was one thing to be bossed around by a guy who was bigger and stronger than me and who had already shown just how he could hurt me. But by this little thing? My pride wouldn't let me just go with it.

"Why should I do what you tell me to?" I said softly. But I wondered if I was playing with fire. This was, after all, the hand that fed.

"Because Tommy wants your vagina to be shaved," she replied, as if that were reason enough. "As I said, don't worry."

I toyed with further rebellion, yet how could I deny that the words 'Tommy' and 'vagina' were having an effect on me? And if she was going to devolve all responsibility for this to the true mastermind behind all this, then it seemed stupid to fight with his messenger. I remembered, too, that I had resolved to try and stay on her good side. And it didn't seem like she wanted to hurt me. Was she on *my* side in some way?

Claire was watching me intently now, her eyes searching my soul. There was no judgement, rather a patient certainty that I would acquiesce. And after another moment of deliberation, I did just that. *Just try to go with it, Laura.*

I went over to the stool, my chain dragging across the floor and my threadbare mattress as I did so. I sat down on it and looked into her greenish-blue eyes. They were really quite bewitching, I had to admit.

Claire brought the bucket and the pouch closer to the stool, knelt down on the ground in front of me and opened the pouch. My breath hitched as I saw that it contained a collection of sharp objects: tweezers, scissors, clippers. I could smell that the pouch was pure leather; the polished metal inside it twinkled.

Her fingers closed around a standard safety razor, and I felt less threatened. The weirdness of what was about to happen hit home, but at least she seemed to be sticking to her word. It was several years since I had been for any kind of waxing or grooming down there. I'd never had the impression it made any difference to George, so I'd stopped. And once I'd gotten out of the habit and work took over my life, I just hadn't found the time anymore. I'd forgotten how bizarre it was to have some woman scratching around between your legs.

Suddenly I felt embarrassed at the bush I'd allowed to run riot down there. No wonder Tommy was displeased.

Displeased? Now that was a funny word my brain just came up with.

"Open your legs, please," said Claire.

I hesitated a moment, then I did as I was told. As I spread my legs, that lust began to coil tighter in my belly. Just when I thought I had calmed my needs from this morning's attack, they were coming back with a vengeance.

Claire showed no signs of emotion, as if this was something she had done many times before. She reached into her pocket and produced a small spray-can of shaving cream. She placed her left hand on my thigh and sprayed a liberal amount of foam onto the patch down at the very bottom of my stomach. Then she took the blade, dipped it into the hot water in the bucket and began to shave me hairless. It wasn't altogether unpleasant. I began to feel cleansed.

I started to trust her too. Was this a chance to get her to open up? Could I learn something?

"You've done this before, haven't you?"

"Oh yes," she said, somehow managing to squeeze a healthy helping of her gorgeous accent into those two syllables. But she didn't elaborate.

"For Tommy?"

"What do you think?" she replied, a note of challenge in her voice.

"I think...I think you do a lot of things for Tommy. And you've done this on other women he has..."

I trailed off. I didn't want to choose the wrong word her.

"Not exactly," she answered, her eyes focused closely on her work. "I do *anything* Tommy wants."

I felt a bizarre twist of excitement as she said that, the cool blade running mere inches from my hungry clitoris.

"Since when?" I asked, trying to keep my voice as even as she did.

"More than 3 years," she replied.

"Oh my," I blurted. The questions blazed in my mind. How did it begin for her? Who were these other women and where were they now? I tried to figure out what to ask first, and how. But she was shutting down now.

"Enough questions," she said. "We are done at the top. I need you to bring your feet up onto the stool. You have space, see? You can lean your back against the wall."

My attention quickly switched back to the physical sensation I was having. The stool was indeed wide enough for me to draw my heels up into a position that would make my current one look positively modest. And this time I didn't notice a murmur of resistance from within.

I wriggled back to create some space, easing my shoulders onto the cool paintwork behind me. Then I pulled first one foot and then the other up onto the stool. I felt like a frog, sitting there like that.

"Okay, put your hands on your knees and keep them there. You need to hold them wide apart. And still. Otherwise I can make a mistake. This is the tricky part now."

I did as instructed. My pussy was now raised to the kneeling French girl's eye level. She had the perfect view and I could not stop myself from blushing. I wanted her to...like what she saw.

She nodded with what looked like satisfaction. Then she looked up at me and, for the very first time, gave me a genuine smile. She didn't need to say anything. Would she...? No, surely not.

Anyway, I wasn't into *that*. It was just this weird situation and the excitement of the morning, that was all.

Yet when Claire sprayed shaving foam on all sides of my opening and then began to spread it carefully around the perimeter of my lips, my breath hitched again. She brushed my clit with her thumb as she smoothed the cream there, and I felt a surge. *Fuck!*

Anytime she moved her head just a little, I could see down her top. I could make out a black bra stretched out across her breasts. Why did I keep on sneaking a peek?

I let her work for a while, trying to control myself. And that was hard when Claire was making no effort to avoid my most sensitive places. She worked with that blade like a surgeon, skating millimetre-close to the bare flesh of my hood. But to do so with such accuracy, she held that hood firm in place with a gentle press of her thumb. My clit cried out and my teeth bit my lip.

She worked her way all the way around my vagina in this fashion. When it came to my opening itself, she gripped the edge between her left thumb and forefingers. Her knuckles fell into my entrance every time. I knew it had to be wet down there. *Dammit Laura, this is not the way to show resistance!*

Claire was impassive and expressionless as she worked her way through my most private zones. Clearly she was not shy of intimate contact with females, but I couldn't see signs of particular enjoyment. What was going through her head right now? And why did I care if she was enjoying it? I looked out of the window, trying to remind myself this was simply a non-sexual, professional procedure. It was impossible to convince myself of that.

Once she had completed a full circuit of my pussy, she produced a cloth from her pocket, dipped it in the warm water and ran it across the whole area where she'd been working. I could feel the leftover shaving cream disappearing and the unmistakable kiss of air on freshly naked skin. She sat back on her heels and surveyed her efforts. She looked pleased with her work.

I decided to venture another question. You feel a certain bond with someone after they've been probing around between your legs for a while. The idea of secrets or barriers between us already seemed more incongruous than when it began.

"Are you also...shaved like this?"

She tore her eyes away from her handiwork, looked up at me and nodded. "Shaved and marked," she said.

"*Marked?* What does that mean?"

She shook her pretty head. "You will find out. It's not my place to tell you. Now please, turn around and lie across the stool. Hands on the floor and legs spread in front of me."

I was shaking now. What was this 'marking' she spoke about? This was starting to sound dangerous again. My mind turned to escape and rebellion, even as I followed her instructions and turned to face the wall. I manoeuvred myself into the awkward position she wanted. Spread-eagled over the stool, my nerves went up another gear as I realized that I wasn't going to be able to see what she did next. Before, I felt a modicum of control over the situation. Now, everything would be a surprise. What was she going to do? Hit me? Burn me?

"Keep very still," she said, pulling my left butt cheek open. I could feel myself blushing at the thought of what she could see in front of her now.

Then came the squish and splash of more shaving cream. And once more the warm, biting touch of the blade. She was working *way* down, around and across that little space between the bottom of my pussy and my actual ass-hole. I tickled deliciously. I wanted to throw my legs wider and slam them shut all at the same time. At least nobody could see the pleasure on my face when I was in this position. I couldn't believe myself.

Claire was making sure to catch every last hair in the territory between my legs. This must be important to someone, I thought, and I was pretty sure I knew who that someone was. I let my eyes close and tried my best not to breathe as she manicured the edges of my anus. I had never had a cosmetic procedure of any description just there, but the consequences of a slip there didn't bear thinking about. But it wasn't at all unpleasant. The precision work managed to tingle some nerves I didn't know I had, that was for sure.

She repeated her trick with the warm cloth. And if I'm honest, I almost asked her for an encore. It was just so comforting to feel that cleansing heat *there*.

"Okay, you are done," she announced suddenly. "You can get up. I will see you later."

I wrestled myself to my feet and watched her as she gathered everything up apart from the stool.

"With food, I hope?" I said in a half-joking tone.

Claire didn't answer. She just gave me a look that said she knew something I didn't.

Chapter XVII

I spent the middle part of the day brooding over the latest developments in my cell. Tommy had used me for his sexual ends and then some equivocal woman had come in and groomed my captured vagina bare, as if in preparation for something.

If I tried to tell myself I hadn't enjoyed the scene with Tommy, it would be a lie. Nor could I pretend the shaving episode with Claire hadn't stirred something unknown within me. And I could hardly ignore the bald, clean feeling between my legs. There was an anticipation in the pit of my stomach that wouldn't die down. I felt like I was in a suspense movie and desperate to find out what happened next.

But I had to remind myself that I was the prisoner of a rampant psychopath. That violent things had already happened, and that they might be only the thin end of the wedge. And then there was the 'marking' Claire had mentioned. It sounded both permanent and painful.

I was beginning to feel more confident that my life itself wasn't in danger. But I was dealing with unpredictable forces, and the sooner I could get out of here, the better. I had to plot some kind of escape. It was time to use my brains.

I wondered if the window was my best chance. I would have to overcome my shyness, yes, but *surely* there was some way to get a message to the outside world through all that glass? But was the glass even transparent from the outside? Now that I thought about it, not many office-style buildings allowed you to see what was going on within.

Could I storm Claire the next time she came in? No, wait, I was in chains. If I could find a way to cut the thing but hide the fact, then I could at least get out of this room. To the elevator, down to the entrance where I'd tried to fight on the first night, then out into the street.

No, wait, I'd be naked. Maybe I could find something to wear somewhere in this building — a maid's outfit in an abandoned cleaning cupboard, perhaps? But I couldn't hang around inside the building for a second if I managed to push my way out of the room. Chances were good that someone — maybe Tommy himself — would see the whole scene via camera. The alarm would be raised right away. And he might not be lurking far away. For all I knew, he was living one floor up or down from here.

Or maybe it was time to forget about clothing. If I could get as far as the street, I would just have to handle it. After three days locked up in here, the prospect of exposure on the street suddenly seemed like a minor inconvenience in comparison to being tied up, beaten...or 'marked'. Maybe being naked in New York would help me attract the attention I needed. I saw myself squatting down in the street outside the building, trying to keep my modesty. If I called out to someone with clothes on, they'd think I was just another loony beggar. But if I was in my birthday suit, surely I'd be too much to ignore? Both men and women would be curious in their own ways.

But it was all moot if I couldn't get out of the chain around my ankle. Even if I found some sort of tool with which to attack it (and nothing came to mind), how could I proceed when I was being watched? It's not like the room even went dark at night.

The more I thought about it, the only way out of my chains was to convince someone to let me go. I had to talk Claire or Tommy into the need for some kind of leg-stretching walkabout. Preferably Claire, because there was no chance I could overpower Tommy — chains or no chains. The other option would be to make him believe I didn't *need* to be kept tied up any more.

I wasn't so sure about the second strategy. Yes, it would give me an endless time window in which to choose my moment, rather than having to do a bump-and-run. And yes, I could definitely imagine an egomaniac like Tommy buying the idea that I wasn't going to try to get away. But it would take a while to get to that point. And what would I have to do to make him swallow my line? How well could I act?

I sat on my mattress as I thought these thoughts, my shoulders propped against the wall. My knees were up and my legs a little open now. Comfort was winning out over modesty. Anyone watching had already seen everything they could possibly see, right? Especially after this morning's shaving demonstration.

Maybe if I attracted more viewers to the internet live stream I felt sure was going on, someone who could rescue me would be among them? Someone from the police?

Or was that just an excuse for me to open my legs and...touch myself? Every time strategizing my escape started to make my head hurt, I allowed that kernel of lust to well up deep inside me. If I let my hand drop to my clit, it wouldn't do the chances of 'Option Two' being viable any harm at all, would it? Was that another excuse? I was so confused. *Fuck this place!*

It was late afternoon when the lights in my cell suddenly dimmed. There hadn't been such a dramatic and sudden change of lighting since I'd first been thrown in here. I sat bolt upright, certain that something was about to happen.

And it did.

The screen in front of me flickered into life. The image upon it was sharp and intense thanks to the low light and what appeared to be excellent resolution. My breath hitched when I saw who stood proud in the middle of the frame: Tommy.

My captor appeared to be standing in the middle of a luxurious hotel suite. Behind him was a large bed covered with a white duvet that looked like fresh-fallen snow. It was dripping with superfluous pillows. in the distance behind him was a sofa and two chairs, all autumnal reds and oranges. Tommy himself was wearing nothing except a ragged but tight-fitting pair of jeans. His arms were folded in front of him.

My eyes took in his steely, bulging torso. That's when I saw his tattoos for the first time. Two horses, prancing intertwined somewhere between fight and play, formed the centrepiece across his chest. The beasts looked wind-battered and proud, their manes untamed. One partly obscured the other, but the aggressive look on the face of the rearmost animal was striking. It looked you right in the eye if you happened to be sizing up Tommy from directly in front.

Not every man can get away with a large tattoo right across his breast. But when your skin is as tight, tanned and hairless as Tommy's it makes for pleasant viewing. And it was by no means the only artwork on his body.

Along his side I could see part of some kind of emblem. If I wasn't mistaken, it portrayed a thistle. It had to be some patriotic crest I didn't completely understand. It made me think of him going into battle for his nation. In my mind he led the army. And riding one of those gleaming stallions.

Across his shoulders and biceps I could see some kind of writing. It was hard to make out much except that they didn't appear to be full words or sentences. Dates? Roman numerals? I would need a closer look to be sure, but they certainly took up their fair share of space. And there was a certain order to them, like seeds sown in a neatly furrowed field.

Tommy looked at the camera for a while. Which meant he was looking at me. Whether he could *actually* see me, I couldn't say. Was this a live broadcast, something akin to a video call or just recording? Yet another gaggle of unknowns. I was learning to brush doubts like that aside. Whatever would happen, would happen.

After a few seconds of ferociously intense gazing, which convinced me that he *could* in fact see me sitting there, Tommy's attention appeared to jump to something beyond the camera. Still right in front of him, but somehow further away. Then he made a beckoning gesture. My muscles reflexed to get up and go towards him, but I stopped myself just in time. How could I go to a man on a screen?

I held my breath and waited. Then somebody emerged from behind the camera and went towards Tommy. Even as the small figure got closer to him, his eyes stared me down. Even when she nudged her body right up against his, wrapping her arms around his midriff and burying the top of her head in his collarbone, he didn't shift his penetrating look.

She didn't have to turn around for me to know exactly who she was, this little fairy clad in nothing but milky-white lingerie. Her stature and that straight blonde hair were enough to tell me the woman's name. A furious jet of jealousy welled up inside of me.

I wanted to turn the fucking screen off from the moment she leapt up to wrap her legs around his waist, his one hand effortlessly supporting her tiny weight. When they began to kiss, I swore I would look away. I was bitter beyond bitter. And I was bitter about being bitter.

But there was no switching *this* device off. And as long as there was no turning it off, I couldn't succeed in looking away either. I was transfixed, as if some awful accident was playing out in front of me. And none of that changed when he turned to one side and threw her down over the end of the bed. Nor when he snapped his fingers — casting a knowing glance in my direction as he did so — and she responded with an instant flip. Now she was bent over double, hands and forehead on the bed and her bare feet spread apart on the royal blue carpet. The horror unfolded in profile before me.

Tommy unbuttoned his jeans and dropped them. His fast-growing cock looked magnificent from side-on. My jaw dropped open just as quickly as my eyes narrowed with bitchy hatred. He used his left hand to shove Claire's panties to one side, leaving her beautiful white underwear otherwise intact. Then, his focus switching entirely to the woman in front of him at last, he rammed his length into her waiting pussy.

Nothing got to me more than the moment Tommy went in. Not because of the entry itself, but because of the way Claire turned her head towards the camera, eyes wide open, and uttered an animal yelp just at the moment he entered her. She wasn't acting — no need for that, I was quite sure — but she knew exactly what she was doing.

She kept on looking my way as she took a violent pounding. I would never have believed I could feel this way, watching this. I should be utterly indifferent, looking for weaknesses I could exploit in my efforts to get out of here. And yet the rapture on her face had me raging.

I was glad Tommy had stopped giving me knowing looks once he got down to business. It was more than enough that Claire kept her gaze on me throughout. Every jerk that convulsed her cute features was like a slap in the face. I raged at myself as much as anybody on the screen.

Finally — inevitably, infuriatingly — Tommy came with a long, growling exhalation. It spoke of nothing but the deep satisfaction of dominance. Claire turned her head away from me, burying it into the linen and convulsing with ecstasy. Did she just come at the same time as him? My head spun at the thought.

Ever the showman, Tommy knew this was the moment to let his actions speak volumes. He didn't give the screen so much as a glance as he drew himself out of Claire and walked towards the camera. He exited stage left, but not before I got a full view of his cock, glistening with her juices.

I wanted to scream out loud.

Chapter XVIII

The screen went black the moment Tommy left the scene. I dropped my head between my knees, a confused jangle of anger and lust. I tried to get my breathing back on track, doing my best to pull myself together and channel my anger in the correct direction. This was not a high-school locker room and I had no time for stupid jealousies. Tommy should be able to screw an army of virgins in front of me without me giving it a second glance. Vile bastards and their whores did *not* deserve my envy.

I had barely three minutes to seethe before Claire appeared in the outer office. I could sense somebody was there even though I was contemplating the insides of my ankles. Clearly it had not taken me long to develop a certain new awareness in this place.

My jaw dropped when I saw her wearing exactly the outfit she'd had on in the pornographic scene I'd just been forced to watch. As she came closer, it was obvious from her just-fucked hair that the broadcast I had just witnessed had been a live one. And her quick arrival meant it must have been filmed real close to here. My theory that there was more going on in this building than just my incarceration had to be correct.

I was used to Claire coming to me with food or some kind of treatment. How was I going to react to her now, glowing as she was and wearing those white bra and panties that I'd never get out of my head? I was deeply emotional so soon after playing witness, and violent punchings played out in my mind's eye. Those nascent thoughts of trying to befriend her — for my own ends or otherwise — were a million miles away.

But punching another woman out of jealousy only made you look stupid. (As if I could look any more stupid than I looked already.) And had she really done anything I wouldn't have done? Wasn't she a victim just like me? I hated the way she had looked at me when he went in, but she might simply have been following instructions. Could he get violent with her as he did with me? I didn't have the answers, but I knew I could *not* allow myself an outburst. An outburst had to serve a calculated purpose to get me out of here. One powered by resentfulness served no such purpose.

I held my breath as she came into the room. I looked past her, not wanting to engage with the crazy hair or the eyes that had just looked at me from the screen. It would not help to look at those things.

"Hello," I said through clenched teeth and clenched fists. She was still coming towards me.

"Hello," she said. Her neutral tone of voice was quiet maddening. *You've just been fucked by Tommy, woman!*

She was advancing towards my mattress. I felt myself tense up as she got nearer. It didn't look like she was going to stop at my feet the way she usually did. She knelt down near my shackled ankle. I cringed, feeling sick to the stomach at the thought of whatever weird surprise was in store.

"Look at me," she said softly.

I took a deep breath, trying not to explode. And very, very slowly I turned my eyes to meet hers. That bewitching colour of sunlit ocean. I said nothing.

"Do you want to be released?"

I felt sure she was teasing me. For the second time in a matter of minutes. I almost spat in her face. I almost hit her with a ton of sarcasm. *But what if she actually means it? Stay cool.*

"I do," I said to her. Wait....did I overdo the indifference just there? I tried to hold her gaze, but it was getting harder to do so. Could I trust this woman? I didn't like searching for an answer in her eyes. I was afraid of the reflections I might see.

"All right then," she said simply. She reached into her panties and produced a small object she must have tucked away in there. It was a key. She deftly unlocked my shackles, freeing me from my bonds.

I stared down at my unencumbered foot, barely able to comprehend that I could get up, walk around...maybe even kick Claire in the face. Who was trusting who here, really?

She stood up and walked towards the door. I didn't move, still waiting for the punchline. I just watched her. This was too easy to be true.

But sure as her word, Claire did not close the door behind her. Just beyond it she turned around and looked at me, the shocked prisoner.

"If you want to go, you can go," she said, gesturing at the door. Then she turned on her heel and walked away from me, that just-fucked hair springing lightly against her shoulders.

"Did Tommy say it was..."

But she had disappeared around the corner before I could finish my question. I could feel I was blushing.

What are you waiting for, Laura? Go!

I shook myself to my senses, got to my feet and walked cautiously towards the door.

And then it hit me. I was still naked.

I hovered on the threshold, my head pounding with doubts.

End of Part 1

Also by James Grey

The Emma Series

In the space of one year, Emma Carling goes from the underpaid slave of a bitchy boss to a wealthy, internationally-famous woman. How? Sex. That's how. But steamy though her journey is, it's far from a simple one.

The three-part *Emma* series, where our male author dares to write erotica from the heroine's point of view, is James Grey's best-known and best-selling series.

You can buy *Escort in Training*, *Escort Unleashed* and *Her Calling* as individual paperbacks. There is also a cost-effective box set digital version of the series.

About James Grey

He may write his erotica under a nom-de-plume, but James Grey has been widely published by magazines and newspapers around the world for the best part of two decades. He still spends much of his working life writing about topics other than hardcore sex. This includes travel books under a different author name.

Grey began writing erotica in the run-up to Christmas 2013, inspired by a recent visit to a sauna in Germany and prompted by a subsequent period of ennui at his aunt's house in France. His self-published author ego was then born on a grim, hung-over New Year's Day in England, when he uploaded *Hot Wet Touches* to the Kindle Store.

He has gone on to become a regular category best-seller on Amazon, and is one of only a small handful of male authors writing erotica. Connect with him online, and you might even find a picture of him the well-travelled Grey at a book signing event.

Grey is in his late thirties and lives in a European capital city. And yes, he likes to keep you guessing. But if you want to know something, why not simply ask him? ;)

Connecting with James Grey

I hope you've enjoyed reading *Out of Office*. Your interest is precious to me as an independent author. Your support, both moral and monetary, keep this whole thing going. There are a hundred ways you can join me on my journey as an author.

For more on how you can get to know me, share feedback and meet other fans, please join the James Grey Fan Group on Facebook. From there, you'll also be able to friend me!

You can also connect with me on MeWe, Goodreads and Twitter (@jamesgreyerotic).

Want me to keep you abreast of any future releases? Send a note to jamesgrey2205@gmail.com, and I'll do just that.

Printed in Poland
by Amazon Fulfillment
Poland Sp. z o.o., Wrocław

60367673R00101